THE COVER GIRL KILLER

When a chartered helicopter plunges into the icy waters of Lake Tahoe, killing its millionaire passenger, what seems a routine claim against a life insurance policy turns into a complex mystery for investigator Hobart Lindsey and his policewoman girlfriend Marvia Plum — for the multimillion-dollar policy is to go to an unnamed model who posed for the cover of an ephemeral mystery paperback in 1951. Lindsey's own life is in danger as he tries to find the now-aged model (if she's still alive!), on a trail full of murder and deception . . .

RICHARD A. LUPOFF

THE
COVER GIRL
KILLER

Complete and Unabridged

LINFORD
Leicester

First published in Great Britain

First Linford Edition
published 2016

A catalogue record for this book is available
from the British Library.

ISBN 978–1–4448–2988–4

Published by
F. A. Thorpe (Publishing)
Anstey, Leicestershire

Set by Words & Graphics Ltd.
Anstey, Leicestershire
Printed and bound in Great Britain by
T. J. International Ltd., Padstow, Cornwall

This book is printed on acid-free paper

Dedication

For my cousin Aaron, who went to
Spain to fight for Democracy, and
who lies in Spanish soil
And for Milton Wolff, who went to
Spain to fight for Democracy
And Esther Miriam Silverstein Blanc,
who went to Spain to nurse those who
fought for Democracy
And returned to tell me their stories

— RAL

1

Hakeem White's skin was dark brown; the other boy's, almost black. The lighter-skinned boy held a fishing rod in one hand and a glittering seven-pound Lake Tahoe salmon in the other. The fish tried to flip free, but he held it tightly. 'Come on, Jamie!'

The darker-skinned boy pointed a Sony Handycam. 'Hold him still, or I can't take your picture.'

Jamie Wilkerson pressed record. The Handycam whirred. The late-afternoon sun glinted off the still surface of Lake Tahoe. The boat, a 28-foot Bayliner, trolled toward the center of the lake, barely maintaining headway.

Over the purr of the engine, a distant *whup-whup-whup* became audible. Jamie swung the Handycam away from his friend and swept it up the snow-covered slopes on the western shore of the lake. An approaching black speck had appeared against the brilliant blue sky.

'Hey!' Hakeem complained. 'You're supposed to be taking my picture. That's just some old heli — '

He stopped as the helicopter seemed to wobble in mid-air. Its familiar *whup-whup-whup* sound developed a sickening syncopation. Hakeem dropped the lake salmon. It flexed the muscles of its silvery tail and launched itself over the stern back into the cold lake. Jamie Wilkerson kept the Handycam focused on the helicopter.

Hobart Lindsey and Marvia Plum, relaxing in the Bayliner's half-open cabin, clambered onto the afterdeck to stand with Marvia's son and his friend. Captain MacKenzie, one hand on the Bayliner's helm, shaded his eyes with the other as he watched the helicopter hover overhead. It shuddered in midair, rotating slowly on its vertical axis, then dropped toward the Bayliner.

MacKenzie yelped and shoved the tourist boat's throttle forward. Its powerful engine responded and the boat leaped ahead. Lindsey grabbed Hakeem and

2

Marvia grabbed Jamie to keep the boys from being flung into the frigid lake. Somehow, Jamie kept the Handycam focused on the helicopter and the record button pressed.

The helicopter splashed down just twenty yards behind the Bayliner. Captain MacKenzie swung his craft in a tight circle and headed back toward the foundering copter. He clicked the boat's Cybernet radio into life and called through to Lake Forest, on Tahoe's north shore, then shoved the Bayliner's gear lever into neutral. The boat slowed as it approached the copter. 'Bart,' he yelled, 'get on the blower — Coast Guard should be coming up. Tell 'em what happened — I have to handle this!' He barreled past the paying passengers and grabbed a downrigger. Marvia pulled the boys aside.

Lindsey had the Coast Guard station on the blower now. 'A helicopter just crashed — it's in the middle of the lake alongside us.'

A voice from the radio said, 'We got a distress call from them. We've got a cutter headed out there now.'

3

'What do you want us to do?'

The voice said, 'Don't go under with the chopper.'

Beyond MacKenzie, Lindsey could see the helicopter foundering deeper into the lake. He thought he could make out two figures inside the glass bubble. Only one of them was moving.

MacKenzie had swung a heavy cable out on the boat's downrigger. He climbed onto the stern gunwale and jumped toward the copter. Chilly water plumed around him. Droplets hit Lindsey's face like icy pellets. MacKenzie struggled to attach the cable to the copter's tail rotor mounting. With a sucking noise, the helicopter disappeared into Lake Tahoe. MacKenzie disappeared, then reappeared, gasping for air, clambering hand-over-hand along the downrigger cable.

Marvia shoved Jamie and Hakeem behind her, toward the Bayliner's cabin. Lindsey had scrambled to the stern of the boat. With Marvia at his side, he stretched his arms over the gunwale as MacKenzie reached it. They grabbed him by the hands, then his arms. He was turning blue, his skin frigid. They managed to haul him over the stern of the boat. He crashed to the deck and crawled toward the cabin, Marvia following.

Lindsey stood in the Bayliner's stern, watching the lake surface where the helicopter had disappeared. The downrigger was playing out cable slowly. The copter was bulky, and it displaced its volume in water, reducing its own weight by an equivalent amount. Bubbles rose from it, bursting when they reached the surface.

Then a hand appeared, then another. Lindsey shouted, 'Someone's alive!'

Marvia, still in her quilted jacket, and Captain MacKenzie, wrapped in a blanket, tumbled back out of the cabin. MacKenzie yelled at the figure who was following his example, clambering hand-over-hand along the downrigger cable. The cable continued to play out, slowing the copter pilot's progress

MacKenzie shoved a boat-hook over the gunwale, and the bedraggled figure released the cable and grabbed it. Lindsey helped MacKenzie haul the boat-hook back while Marvia grabbed the survivor's arm and pulled him over the gunwale. Lindsey saw that one of his legs stuck out from its socket at a crooked angle.

As Marvia tried to hustle the dripping man into the cabin, he screamed and collapsed. Lindsey realized that his leg was broken in several places. He scrambled to help Marvia with the man, dragging him on his back into the cabin and wrapping him in a blanket.

Captain MacKenzie picked up the ship-to-shore microphone and shouted at the Coast Guard. Jamie pointed the Handycam at the Coast Guard cutter approaching from the north.

The injured man shook his head, shoving himself upright on his elbow. He yelled, 'I've got to get Mr. Vansittart out of there!'

MacKenzie shoved past them and peered into the lake, studying the downrigger. The cable had paid out to its end, revealing a polished metal reel. Lindsey could feel the Bayliner tilting. MacKenzie roared, 'We're going to founder!' He tugged the heavy downrigger from its mounting. It whipped into the air, missing MacKenzie by fractions, then arced over the Bayliner's stern and splashed beneath the surface after the helicopter.

The survivor lay on his back, moaning. 'It was Mr. Vansittart! I tried to get him out but I couldn't!'

The Coast Guard cutter hove to alongside the Bayliner. A guardsman called, 'We're going to throw you a line, Bayliner. We'll tow you to safety.'

MacKenzie shook his head. 'I don't need a tow. *He* does.' He pointed at the lake, where the helicopter and its passenger had disappeared. 'But I've got a badly injured man on board. I'm heading for port. He needs to get to the hospital.'

$\star$ $\star$ $\star$

Hobart Lindsey, Marvia and the two boys sat on the edge of the big bed. All had showered and changed into warm clothes. They were watching CNN with the sound muted, waiting for Jamie's fifteen seconds

7

of fame. Hakeem was not very happy that Jamie had held the camcorder and not him.

'I'm going to be a TV newsman when I grow up,' Jamie enthused. I've already got a start and a check coming, too.'

Marvia hushed the two boys. 'Look.' She hit the mute button and the sound came back on. A talking head in the studio of CNN's Reno affiliate was jabbering at the camera. The image on the screen cut to Jamie's footage, starting with a flash of Hakeem's grinning face and his lake salmon, then panning away to the tiny speck of the copter.

The studio announcer said, 'These remarkable pictures were taken by a ten-year-old boy, Jamie Wilkerson, of Berkeley, California, vacationing at Lake Tahoe with his mother and best friend. The helicopter ran into trouble as it began to cross the lake en route from its passenger's Belmont, California home to a destination in Reno.'

On the TV screen the helicopter was seen to fall toward the lake. Almost miraculously, Jamie had kept the Handy-cam image steady and clear. Maybe the boy did have a future as a cameraman.

'The pilot, John Frederick O'Farrell of Mountain View, California, is a Vietnam veteran who operates a private air-taxi service. He was rushed to Doctors' Hospital in Truckee and is in intensive care, suffering from a compound fracture of the leg and internal injuries. Doctors are guardedly optimistic regarding O'Farrell's condition. Coast Guard authorities at Lake Tahoe said that only the quick action of Captain Kevin MacKenzie of the Bayliner *Tahoe Tailflipper* saved O'Farrell's life.'

The screen showed O'Farrell climbing out of the lake, Marvia hauling him by one dripping sleeve while O'Farrell clung to the boat-hook that MacKenzie and Lindsey had passed to him. On the video tape, the injuries to O'Farrell's leg were horrifyingly obvious.

Then the image cut to a still picture of a white-haired business-suited man. The surroundings were unquestionably an office. The announcer furnished a voice-over. 'Albert

9

Crocker Vansittart was the last scion of a pioneer California family. A confirmed bachelor, Vansittart inherited a fortune estimated at fifty million dollars and ran its worth up to ten times that amount. A lifelong resident of Belmont, Vansittart was traveling to Reno on holiday.'

The scene cut back to Lake Tahoe. The news network must have hired its own helicopter and had it hover over the crash site. Now it was night-time; the footage must have been shot within the past hour. A Coast Guard cutter had returned and its crew were working by floodlight, dropping lines into the black water. They hauled them back without results.

The announcer introduced a professor of marine geology from the University of Nevada at Reno. 'Lake Tahoe is more than a quarter of a mile deep,' the professor intoned. 'Once you get past the surface layers, the temperature is a uniform forty degrees Fahrenheit, year round. We don't really know what lies at the bottom of the lake — or who. But you can be sure, if anybody rode that helicopter to the bottom of the lake, he isn't alive now.'

'Haven't you tried this technique before, Professor, looking for Tahoe Tessie?'

'A lot of people laugh at Tessie and call her our own version of the Loch Ness Monster. But we've found some amazing species in recent decades. Why, no one believed that a live coelacanth could possibly be swimming around today, until . . . '

Lindsey jumped when the telephone rang at his elbow. As he picked up the handset he glanced at his watch: 11:30 p.m. It had been a long day and evening, but everyone, including the ten-year-olds, was too energized to sleep.

'Stand by for Mr. Richelieu.' Lindsey grimaced.

Richelieu said, 'Lindsey, I'm surprised you're still awake.' He sounded like Jack Nicholson on valium, Lindsey thought. 'You're not watching CNN by any chance, are you, Lindsey?'

'As a matter of fact, I am.'

'Do you know who died this afternoon?'

'You mean Albert Crocker Vansittart?'

'Correct. That was you and your girlfriend in that boat, right?'

'Yes, the *Tahoe Tailflipper*.'

'Well, Hobart Lindsey, International Surety's hero *du jour*, I don't know how you always manage to land in hot water, but you're in it again.'

Lindsey had carried the telephone as far away from the TV as he could, closed himself in the bathroom with the cord snaked under the door. The lodge didn't have cordless phones in case guests carried them away like souvenir towels.

'I don't understand, Mr. Richelieu. Why am I in this? What does this have to do with International Surety? What does it have to do with SPUDS?' And why, Lindsey wondered, had the director of the Special Projects Unit/Detached Service tracked him down to a lakeside lodge in Tahoe City long after business hours?

'Good thing Mrs. Blomquist and I were working late tonight and happened to turn on the set here in the office.'

Lindsey didn't rise to that one.

'Vansittart had one of our flag policies.

12

I assume the coroner out there is going to certify that he's dead.'

'Without a body, Mr. Richelieu?'

'Come on, Lindsey. Enough witnesses saw that copter crash. Including you of all people. And it's on tape. And the pilot says it was Vansittart.'

'Okay. Vansittart had an International Surety policy?'

'Four million dollars' worth.'

'Four — four *million*?'

'That's right. Been paying in on it since 1951. Biggest life policy I.S. ever wrote.'

'Well . . . well . . . I guess we'll just have to pay off, then. If they can recover the body. Or, ah, once the coroner certifies that he's dead. I don't suppose we can wait seven years?'

'Not seven years. And no double indemnity, either. I looked. Give thanks for small blessings.'

'I still don't see why you called me, Mr. Richelieu. I'm on vacation this weekend. That's a huge policy, and the death of the insured will have to be certified, but it still sounds like a job for the nearest branch office. Why don't they just enter the event through KlameNet and — '

'You aren't listening, Lindsey. This is a *flag* policy, understand? And there's something peculiar about it, aside from the circumstances of Vansittart's death.'

'What's peculiar about Vansittart's policy?'

'The beneficiary. Cripes, I'd never write a policy like this one. I don't care who the insured was; I don't care how much he was paying in premiums.'

Lindsey did not ask who the beneficiary was. He waited.

'The beneficiary is the woman on the cover of *Death in the Ditch*.'

'You're kidding.'

'Lindsey, I hand-picked you out of that crummy little office you were in. I gave you your big break in this company. You know I don't kid.'

'Right. So who's the woman on the cover of *Death in the Ditch*?'

'That's what International Surety is paying you to find out.'

'Sounds like a book. Kind of like that porn star who posed for the baby-food label or the soap-flakes package or whatever it was. But *Death in the Ditch* sounds like a book.'

'Find out, Lindsey. And find the woman. We owe her three million dollars.'

'I thought you said four million?'

'I told you this was a flag policy. If we find the woman and pay the benefits, International Surety gets a twenty-five percent finder's fee. That's a cool million smackers.'

'And if we don't find her? I mean, this sounds like a long shot if the policy was written in 1951. She may not even be alive. What happens if we can't find her? Or if she's deceased?'

'If we can't find her, or if she's deceased, the money goes to something called the World Fund for Indigent Artists. Sounds like Vansittart was hung up on artists and models. Wouldn't be the first.'

'And you want me to find the woman. How long do we have?'

'Policy doesn't specify. But we have to notify the artists' fund, and once they smell four million bucks, they're going to start pressing us hard.'

'And there's no finder's fee.'

'That's right, Lindsey. I swear, young feller, if you keep on showing your smarts like you been, you've got a bright future with this company.'

'I'll get on it first thing Monday morning, Mr. Richelieu.'

'You'll get on it first thing *tomorrow*, bucko. In fact, suppose you get on it tonight. You've got your company palm-top with you?'

'I have it.'

'To work, then. You're not on an hourly wage, Lindsey. To work.'

Lindsey opened the bathroom door. He could see Jamie and Hakeem silhouetted against the TV screen. They'd lost interest in CNN and switched channels to a Japanese monster movie.

Lindsey quietly placed the telephone handset on its base. The boys did not budge. He pulled on his goose-down jacket and motioned to Marvia. She slipped into her own jacket and followed him onto the wooden walkway outside their room.

The lodge was separated from the lake

by a broad lawn covered with drifted snow. The January moon reflected off the lake's smooth surface. The Coast Guard cutter had apparently returned to its pier and the news helicopter to its base. Across the lake, a torchlight ski party was visible as a cluster of tiny moving sparks.

Marvia said, 'We have to go back, don't we?'

He nodded.

'It was going so well. Like a real family.' She looked angry. 'How did your boss know where we were?'

Lindsey told Marvia about Richelieu and Mrs. Blomquist working late and just happening to turn on a TV in the office. 'He must have had her calling every hotel and lodge at the lake 'til she found us.'

Marvia grinned bitterly. 'We should have registered as the Smith family.'

Lindsey looked down at Marvia's face. The moon reflected from her dark eyes like two bright disks. 'Let's chase the boys into their own room. I can log onto the 24-hour inter-library net from my palm-top. Give me an hour or so, then we can turn in.'

2

Since Lindsey had moved from International Surety's Walnut Creek office to SPUDS, he could pretty well set his own days and hours. Marvia Plum, on the other hand, as a homicide sergeant on the Berkeley Police Department, had to be available when the department needed her. But this time it was Lindsey who had got the call, and this time it was Lindsey who did as he was commanded: *Find the woman on the cover of* Death in the Ditch.

He dropped Marvia and both youngsters at her house. She would take care of them, get Hakeem White back to his parents', and take her own son to her parents' house. They would spend the evening there. Marvia spent more time with her mother since her father's death. Not that Gloria Plum needed it; she had always been an island unto herself. But somehow, it seemed to Lindsey, Marvia drew strength from being in the house where she was raised, and where her father had lived almost until the end.

Lindsey left them at Oxford Street in Berkeley. Marvia would drive Jamie and Hakeem to Bonita Street in her classic Mustang.

Lindsey's computer search had turned up scores of books with *Death in* in their titles. There was *Death in the Devil's Acre* by Anne Perry, 1985, and there was *Death in the Diving Pool* by Carol Carnac, 1940. That was where *Death in the Ditch* belonged, right between them. But it wasn't there.

But what would have a cover with a woman on it, with a title like *Death in the Ditch*, other than a book? A magazine? A record album? A pack of trading cards? Vansittart's life policy had been issued in 1951. If the designated beneficiary hadn't been changed in later years, that would narrow the field.

Lindsey headed for Walnut Creek. He pulled his rebuilt Volvo 544 into the driveway and parked beside the silver-gray Oldsmobile that had been parked there increasingly often these past few months.

Inside the house he found Mother's new friend, Gordon Sloane, sitting in the living room with his shoes off and a nearly full martini glass in his hand. He looked at Lindsey in surprise.

'I thought you were up in Tahoe. Your mother said — '

Before Lindsey could answer, Mother came into the room. Her hair had gone to gray — every time Lindsey noticed a change in her it was a shock to him — and she carried a wooden salad bowl and a pair of hinged tongs. Lindsey embraced her and planted a kiss on her cheek.

'I guess you two were planning an evening at home. I can make myself scarce.'

Mother smiled. 'We wouldn't throw you out of your own home. There's plenty of food.'

At dinner he told them about the events at Tahoe, and about Desmond Richelieu's telephone call.

Sloane said, 'We caught part of the

report on TV. It was in this morning's papers, too. They're going nuts over Vansittart. I didn't realize you were involved.'

After dinner was over and the dishes cleaned and put away, Mother turned on the TV. The evening news was just coming on. There was a follow-up to the Vansittart story. The Coast Guard had dropped a plumb line, trying to find the helicopter. Nothing came up. The lake was too deep at that point, and the line couldn't even reach the bottom.

There was a canned biography of Vansittart. Black-and-white footage showed the millionaire toasting the mayor of San Francisco at some civic dinner, and shaking hands with the governor of California at another. Vansittart had apparently been an ambassador to several postage-stamp nations in the 1960s and '70s, obviously the reward for generous campaign donations to the presidents of that era.

And newsreel footage of Vansittart escorting movie stars to premieres and rolling dice at the gaming tables in Reno and Las Vegas. Quite a fellow. The reporter in Reno mentioned that Vansittart had been traveling by chartered helicopter to his planned seventy-fifth birthday party when the copter crashed and sank into Lake Tahoe.

*   *   *

In the morning the Oldsmobile was still in the driveway. Lindsey got into his Volvo and headed downtown to the International Surety office. He still preferred to work out of the office where he'd worked for so many years.

Not that the atmosphere was perfect. Elmer Mueller, Lindsey's successor as area manager, was a loathsome bigot, and Mueller's hand-picked office manager, Kari Fielding, was as vicious as her boss. But in a strange way Lindsey enjoyed seeing them once in a while; it made him appreciate the rest of his life.

But it was Saturday and he was alone in the office. Agent claims would be filed directly through KlameNet. Anything else could wait until Monday morning.

Lindsey used the office computer to log onto the mainframe at National. He printed out the text of Vansittart's policy, checked the history file, and verified that the peculiar description of the beneficiary had been there from the outset. The only changes over the years had come about when the alternate bennie had changed its name. Originally the Chicago Artists and Models Mutual Aid Society, it had now become the World Fund for Indigent Artists. The current address was 101 California Street, San Francisco. Lindsey knew the building well: a gleaming modern high-rise full of high-profile law firms and corporate offices.

The current President of WFIA was one Roger St. John Cooke. Vice President was Cynthia Cooke. It sounded like a nice little mom 'n' pop nonprofit foundation. The world was full of do-gooders, including those who did well by doing good.

Lindsey made a note to expect some input from the Cookes. There would be a polite phone call, then a lawyer letter. But Lindsey wasn't going to worry too much about the contingent bennies today. He shut down the computer, left the office, grabbed a snack downstairs and walked to his car.

He parked in a city garage just off Telegraph Avenue and headed for Cody's, the town's premiere bookstore. A clerk at the center desk offered to help him. He asked if she knew of a book called *Death in the Ditch*. No author, no publisher, but it was probably first issued in 1951 or so. The clerk smiled. 'I doubt that it's still in print, unless it was a classic of some kind.'

'I don't know what kind of book it was, except there was a woman on the cover. I'm afraid I've never seen it.'

The clerk turned away. Over her shoulder she said, 'I'll look in *Books in Print*.' She punched some keys on a computer. Mysterious boxes and symbols raced across the monitor screen. The clerk turned back to Lindsey. 'Sorry. Doesn't show anything like that.'

Lindsey had one hand on the counter, and the clerk put hers on top of his. 'Maybe you could try Moe's next door.

First floor, they have a lot of used paperbacks. That might be your best bet.'

Lindsey thanked her and walked next door. The clerk was right; Moe's had thousands of used paperbacks. Trouble was, they were arranged by author, not title.

But again a clerk came to the rescue. 'You know the San Francisco Mystery Book Store? Twenty-fourth Street? If anybody can help you, they can.'

At Twenty-fourth Street he found a parking place and walked to the mystery specialty store. The place was crammed with books and book lovers. He squeezed through narrow aisles and reached the upstairs room. Hardcovers and paperbacks were intermixed. There must be thousands of them. If Lindsey had been a mystery fan, he would have been in paradise.

But again, the arrangement was alphabetical by author, not title. He squeezed back down the narrow staircase. A blonde woman with sharp, attractive features sat at a tiny, battered desk. Lindsey asked her if she knew of a book called *Death in the*

Ditch, published around 1951.

The woman frowned. 'I've never heard of it. You know anything about it?'

'Only that there was a woman on the cover.'

She said, 'You sure of that? Cover, not jacket?'

'I've never seen it.'

'Then it's probably a paperback. There weren't as many published back in the early '50s before Bantam got going, then Ballantine and Ace. But '51 — there were some pretty ephemeral outfits around then.' She looked up at Lindsey. 'What you really ought to do is, you ought to talk to Scotty Anderson. You know him?'

'Afraid not.'

'Great collector. If you need an old paperback, if anybody in the world has it, Scotty does. You want his address, phone number?'

Lindsey did. He flipped his pocket organizer open and jotted down the information she gave him. 'He won't mind my calling?'

'Just tell Scotty I sent you.' The blonde

told Lindsey her name and he added that to the organizer.

After thanking her, he headed for a pay phone. Anderson was at home. Lindsey made an appointment for Sunday afternoon and hung up. Maybe he was getting somewhere.

Wanting to speak to Marvia, he tried her mother's house. Gloria Plum answered. Marvia had taken her son and his friend to the mall to make up for their canceled snow weekend. Somehow Gloria managed to blame Lindsey for the canceled weekend.

This is really swell, Lindsey thought. *I'm not even married and I've got mother-in-law problems already.* He went home.

Mother had planned to go out for the evening with Gordon Sloane. They'd been dating for almost a year now. They'd met when Mother got a job — her first real, out-of-the-home job, at Sloane's company, Consolidated Alpha. Sloane worked in product development. Mother was a secretary, not a bad job for a woman entering the job market for the first time in her late fifties.

Lindsey had never been able to learn what products Sloane developed. Consolidated Alpha was one of those shadowy Bay Area corporations that seemed to have something to do with the University of California, or maybe some government agency.

Lindsey fixed himself some dinner, then went for a walk around the block. Mother had spoken of marriage to Sloane, selling the house and buying a condo. Lindsey had asked Marvia to marry him enough times, and she seemed to be edging, very slowly, toward doing it. His comfortable life in the nest looked as if it were coming to an end.

When he got home there was still no sign of Mother; no silver-gray Oldsmobile in the driveway. He showered and climbed into bed.

★   ★   ★

The next day, Sunday, Lindsey kept his appointment with Scotty Anderson. Anderson lived in Castro Valley, an apartment in a standard, low-rise, 1970s development. The neighborhood was marked with strip-malls and broad, treeless streets. The parking lot outside the apartment was full of ten-year-old Toyotas and deteriorating pickup trucks.

Lindsey rang the bell beside Anderson's door. Anderson was massive, with uncombed mouse-brown hair, and looked like he had shopped with taste and care at Goodwill. When he greeted Lindsey, he felt as if his hand was being absorbed by a great, soft animal.

The inside of Anderson's apartment was a combination library, museum and shrine. The air outside might be cold and damp in winter and hot and dry in summer; inside Scotty Anderson's apartment it was kept at a steady temperature and humidity. The Library of Congress had nothing on Scotty Anderson.

'So you're doing some research on paperbacks.' Anderson put one bear-like hand on Lindsey's shoulder while he closed the outside door with the other. 'Come on in. Let me show you around.'

Lindsey had never seen a residence so

jammed with books. The walls were covered with shelving packed with books. The room was divided into narrow passageways, little more than tunnels, between rows of standing metal shelves. Books were everywhere. The ends of the rows were covered with posters advertising books, blowups of ads for books, reproductions of covers of books. Ninety-nine percent of them were paperbacks.

Anderson led Lindsey up one aisle and down the next, declaiming on cover artists, publishers, authors, points of distinction between different editions. Lindsey's head was soon swimming.

Finally they reached a cramped room furnished as an office. Anderson gestured Lindsey to a battered wooden chair. He dropped his own bulk into another. There was a computer on the desk, a stack of reference books beside the computer and a row of file cabinets beside the desk.

Anderson looked at Lindsey expectantly. 'Death in the Ditch.' He grinned. 'Lovisi sent you, right?'

'Who's Lovisi?'

'Come on, I know I'm a little late, but

does he want it fast or does he want it right? This ain't easy. What did you say your name was? I know most of the collectors, but you don't look familiar.'

'We've never met.'

'The draft is done. I'm really sorry; he's been patient and I appreciate it. Another week. Two at the most.'

'I'm afraid you misunderstand. I'm with International Surety.' Lindsey reached for his wallet. Anderson flinched, then relaxed as Lindsey handed him a business card. 'You see, there's been a death. You may have heard about it. Albert Crocker Vansittart.'

Anderson waited.

'His helicopter crashed in Lake Tahoe. The pilot survived, but Mr. Vansittart was lost. They're going to try and find the wreckage. The University of Nevada is sending a team with fiber-optic equipment.'

Anderson nodded. 'I heard something about that on the car radio.'

Okay, at least the guy had some awareness of the outside world. 'My company had issued a policy on Mr.

Vansittart's life. He hasn't been formally declared dead as yet — that's going to be a little problem. Who has jurisdiction? And of course there's no body as yet.'

Anderson frowned. 'This is all fascinating stuff, but what does it have to do with me? You sure Lovisi didn't send you to pressure me?'

Lindsey sighed. 'I promise you, Mr. Anderson, I haven't an idea in the world who this Lovisi person is.'

'Okay.' Anderson stood up. 'But if Lovisi didn't send you, how do you know about *Death in the Ditch*?'

'It was in Vansittart's life policy. It names his beneficiary as the woman on the cover of *Death in the Ditch*.' Lindsey was going to say more, but the dawning light of comprehension had brightened Scotty Anderson's face like an interior sun.

'Poor Lovisi. I'm going to have to revise the article, I can see that.'

Lindsey frowned.

'Gary Lovisi runs *Paperback Parade*. It's a collector's journal.'

'For people who collect paperbacks,'

Lindsey supplied.

'An interesting character. When he started out, his stuff was so crude I couldn't believe it. Like he was the Ed Wood of publishing. But he kept at it and now he turns out beautiful stuff.'

Lindsey waited patiently for Anderson to go on.

'I promised Lovisi an article for *Paperback Parade* on the legendary Paige Publications. Everybody in the hobby claims he knows somebody who has some Paige books, even claims he's seen one. But none of them turn up at the shows; none of them turn up in dealers' catalogs.'

'Do they really exist?'

Anderson's pale blue eyes lost their wide innocence. 'I have one,' he whispered.

3

Anderson heaved his bulk out of his wooden chair and invited Lindsey to follow him. They paraded through a warren of metal shelves until they came to a gunmetal door with a huge combination lock. Anderson crouched, hiding the lock from Lindsey's view.

Anderson swung the heavy door open to reveal a closet-sized safe. It was filled with metal boxes. He ran his finger across the rows of boxes, all marked with index numbers. Finally he pulled down a box, opened it, and extracted a transparent envelope containing a paperback book. He held the book toward Lindsey. 'Hold this.'

Lindsey did. What kind of person would maintain this level of security on what was obviously a treasure, yet hand it so casually to a stranger? But Lindsey had been working with collectors for years, and nothing they did could surprise him now.

Like Alice following the white rabbit, he was led to a living room, or what must pass for one in this bizarre apartment. There were actually a few square feet of wall space not covered with books. Instead, framed paintings had been hung. They were well-executed, but they didn't have the feel of gallery paintings. There were scenes of gangsters blasting at uniformed police, spaceships silhouetted against blazing multicolored suns and planets, gorgeous women in low-cut gowns lounging against pianos, cowpokes galloping straight out of the frame.

Anderson beamed at Lindsey's expression. 'You like them? Originals!'

'They look like movie posters. Very vivid.'

'They're paperback cover paintings. Look, that's a Mitchell Hooks. That's a Bob Maguire. And that beauty is — ' He pointed. ' — a Robert McGinnis. You won't see many of those. And that red one with the spaceman and the bat-creatures is a Frank R. Paul. No, they don't paint 'em the way they used to.'

'They must be valuable.'

'You wouldn't believe it. Five or six figures. They used to throw them away back in the fifties. Listen, if I just had a time machine, what I couldn't do!'

Lindsey had to get the subject back to *Death in the Ditch*. 'You said something about . . . ' He gestured to the book in Anderson's hand.

Anderson slid the envelope across his desk. 'Please don't open it. If you need to look at the book, I'll get it out for you. It must be done just right or it can be damaged.'

Lindsey leaned over the book. It was entitled *Buccaneer Blades*. The author was Violet de la Yema. The cover illustration could have been straight out of a '50s pirate movie starring Burt Lancaster and Maureen O'Hara, with Basil Rathbone as the evil Spanish governor of a Caribbean island and Akim Tamiroff as his comic aide.

He turned the book over carefully. 'No price?'

'They were all a quarter. No need for a price back then. Did you catch the publisher's logo?'

'I see it there in the corner. Nice idea — the open book with all the pages, and the publisher's name, Paige.'

Lindsey turned the book over. The spine was printed in black with the title and byline dropped out, in white. The Paige Publications logo was reproduced at the base of the spine, along with a serial number, 101. Lindsey raised his eyebrows. 'Does 101 mean this was the very first Paige book?'

'Apparently it does. Nobody really knows much about Paige. Paiges are the holy grail of paperback collectors. Like the first ten Pocket Books. They printed 10,000 of each, so you'd think there would be a lot of them left. Well, except for *Enough Rope* by Dorothy Parker; for some reason they only did 7,600. But they're scarcer than hen's teeth. People must have read 'em and thrown 'em away. Or the LA Bantams. If you could get hold of *The Shadow and the Voice of Murder* or *Tarzan in the Forbidden City* . . . '

Lindsey said, 'I've worked on a comics

collectibles case before, but this field is new to me.'

'You ought to read one of the books on the subject. Thom Bonn's, or Piet Schreuders'. Anyway, if you know anything about collectibles, you know that their intrinsic value doesn't really matter. What's the difference between two identical books, only one of them has a minor typo in it and the other doesn't, and we know that the typo was only in the true first edition and corrected after that?'

'I — ' Lindsey hesitated.

'It makes all the difference in the world,' Anderson went on. 'It's the difference between a treasure and a reading copy. It's the difference between a book to kill for and one you can pick up at any lawn sale for a nickel.' Anderson's predatory grin returned. 'Matter of fact, I got my Paige at a garage sale in Lafayette. Just cruising, stopped to see what they had. All the usual junk, last season's Robert Ludlum, fifteenth printing, couple of Agatha Christies and Ellery Queens, zillionth editions, and . . . and a Paige!'

Lindsey nodded. He understood collectors as well as anyone could who was not himself a collector.

'I asked where the book came from,' Anderson continued, 'after I'd bought it, of course. Nobody knew. Maybe Grandma read it when she was a girl. She always kept it, the old dear. But she's gone to Valhalla now, and they were cleaning out her room, and nobody in the family really wanted Grandma's old paperbacks, so — out they went. For a nickel apiece.' Anderson cackled gleefully at the thought of his great coup. 'One thing that I haven't been able to verify, though.'

'What's that?'

'The book is autographed. That is, *somebody* wrote a message in it. No, don't open it up, please. I remember exactly what it says. *To my Comrade with thanks. Salud y suerte. Violeta.* That's health and luck in Spanish. But nobody knows what Violet de la Yema's handwriting looks like. And why 'Violeta' instead of 'Violet' or 'Vi?' So — is it an authentic inscription?' Anderson shrugged. 'I like to think it is. But nobody can tell me.'

Lindsey let his eye settle on the deep cleavage of the model on the front of *Buccaneer Blades*, then turned the book over. He could feel his heart shift into overdrive. The back cover of *Buccaneer Blades* was not devoted to a blurb extolling the virtues of the book, or a paragraph lifted from a particularly steamy scene, as he'd expected. Instead, it featured an ad for another Paige book. It was an ad for *Death in the Ditch*!

The copy read like a standard hard-boiled mystery — a struggling, penniless private eye, a one-armed bartender ('He'd left his grenade-hurling wing on the bloody coral of Tarawa'), a gorgeous babe ('Smoldering eyes and gams like Grable's'), murderous mobsters ('The Big Guy was gone and they were ready to kill for a piece of his empire'), and corrupt cops ('They were there to enforce the law, but the law they enforced was written in dollars — and hot lead').

It sounded like something written in the late 1940s rather than the early '50s. That one-armed bartender was the giveaway. By the early 50s, Tarawa was yesterday's story, along with Iwo Jima and Saipan and Guadalcanal and the rest of the island-hopping battles of the Pacific campaign. World War II was stale news.

Lindsey had to squint to make out the by-line on the miniature cover of *Death in the Ditch* — Del Marston.

It looked as if finding Albert Crocker Vansittart's beneficiary was going to take some serious detecting. Maybe old Del Marston, the author of *Death in the Ditch*, would have had his hero solve the puzzle with a gat and a few slugs of bourbon, but Lindsey didn't work that way. The job could be laborious and time-consuming.

He hoped no one else had got there first and erased all the clues. Lindsey was a good investigator, but he was no magician. He asked Anderson, 'Would you take the book out of the envelope for me? Please?'

Anderson's huge hand slowly peeled back a strip of tape, opened a transparent flap and slid the book gently from its reliquary. He held it toward Lindsey, but his look said: *don't touch.*

'Have you actually read *Buccaneer Blades*?'

'No way. Much too fragile. I did open it far enough to shoot the indicia and front matter, and the first couple of pages. It's routine Spanish Main stuff.'

'Do you think you could open it for me? So I could copy down the publisher's address, and the like.'

Anderson shook his head. 'Don't want to risk it. But you can have copies of my printouts. I'll get 'em for you before you leave.' He slid the book back into its transparent envelope, sealed the envelope with tape once more, and laid it on a low table. He leaned back in his chair, his hands behind his head. He'd shown his treasure, and his visitor had been clearly and suitably impressed. It was a good day for Scotty.

'I only found this Paige a couple of months ago. Nobody has one. I went to the Library of Congress to check on it, and they don't have any Paiges that they know of.'

That surprised Lindsey. 'I thought

42

— you know, for copyright registration under the old law — wouldn't they have sent copies there?'

Anderson nodded. 'The books were registered, okay. That's why I have a list of all the Paiges, or at least all the ones that they registered. The serial numbers jibe, though, so I think that's all. But they don't have any copies. A lot of old paperbacks and magazines just got shoved in a back room, and they're still there. They'll shelve them when they get a chance, they say, but they never get around to it. But how's this — it looks as if some Congressmen were pretty interested in the Paige books, and they leaned on the library staff to log 'em in so they could check 'em out. They were checked out by a HUAC staffer — you know about HUAC?'

'Uh — '

'House Committee on Un-American Activities. Run by a couple of Congressional lice named Martin Dies and J. Parnell Thomas. Sort of premature Joe McCarthyites. Tricky Dickie Nixon got his start with HUAC.'

Lindsey wasn't going to talk about Richard Nixon. Instead he asked, 'Why would they want these particular books?'

'That's what I wondered. I think I have a good clue, although it might take some more digging in the *Congressional Record* to find out for sure.'

'But if the books were in the Library of Congress, aren't they still there?'

Anderson grinned. 'You'd be amazed how many books get checked out by members of Congress. They wouldn't lower themselves to deal with mere librarians, of course. They send staff people, generally low-level staff people. They check things out and they never give them back. I mean, what's going to happen? Somebody in the library calls up Senator Jones and says, 'You have our first edition *Maltese Falcon*; you better return it or there's a nickel fine for every day it's late' — huh? Fat chance.'

'You said you had a clue?'

Anderson shoved himself upright. 'You wait here.' He picked up his precious copy of *Buccaneer Blood* and headed for the door.

When Anderson returned he had disposed of *Buccaneer Blood*; probably locked it away in its reliquary. He was carrying a few sheets of computer printout.

'This is my article for *Paperback Parade*. Just a draft; I have to work on it some more. Especially with this insurance story of yours.'

After seating himself, he selected one sheet of paper and handed it to Lindsey. 'This is a complete Paige Publications bibliography. There might have been some that they didn't register, but I think that's unlikely.'

The heading on the page gave Paige Publications' address: Paige Building, LaSalle at Kinzie Streets, Chicago, Illinois. There were three columns of type on the page. Lindsey scanned them carefully.

Buccaneer Blood
Violet de la Yema   1951
Cry Ruffian!
Salvatore Pescara   1951
Death in the Ditch
Del Marston   1951

Teen Gangs of Chicago a.k.a.
  Al Capone's Heirs
(anonymous)   1951
By Studebaker Across America
Walter Roberts   1952
Great Baseball Stars of 1952
J. B. Harkins   1952
I Was a Lincoln Brigadier
Bob Walters   1952
Prisoner! ('by the author of *Teen
  Gangs of Chicago*')   1952

Lindsey looked up from the list. 'Why would a Congressional committee care about these books? What difference does a pirate swashbuckler make, or a book about gangsters, or a Studebaker trip, for heaven's sake?'

Anderson extended a thick finger and tapped the paper in Lindsey's hands. 'There's the one. That's the one I think got their backs up.' He pointed at the line for *I Was a Lincoln Brigadier*. 'You know about the Abraham Lincoln Brigade?'

'I think it rings a faint bell.'

'American volunteers, fought in the Spanish Civil War, 1936. They went there

46

to fight fascism, to fight against Franco. They figured he was a front man for Hitler, and they weren't too far from right.'

'What's wrong with that?'

'Well, there was a lot of communist influence in the Lincolns. Hell, there were a lot of communists in there. But they went to Spain to fight the fascists. At least that was their version. But once the cold war got going, these guys were highly suspect. Highly suspect. So, when Bob Walters brought out his little book, HUAC jumped up and down and started doing its war dance.'

'Do you mind if I keep this list?' Lindsey asked.

'Feel free, I've got it all in my computer.'

Lindsey got to his feet. 'You've been very helpful. If you want to bill us, International Surety will pay a modest honorarium.'

Anderson waved that away. 'Glad to have a chance to show off my collection a little bit. Better let me show you the way out. People have got lost in this place and starved to death.'

As Lindsey started toward his Volvo, he heard Anderson's door open behind him. 'Mr. Lindsey?' he called.

Lindsey stopped and turned around.

'You're sure Lovisi didn't send you?'

He managed not to laugh. 'I'm sure.

'Funny.' Anderson frowned. 'I had a note from Lovisi last week saying that somebody else was interested in the Paige stuff. Said he was a serious researcher; claimed that he was some kind of professor or something.'

'Have you heard from this person?'

'No way. Lovisi wouldn't do that. Let the bozo do his own work. I don't mind helping you, Mr. Lindsey — you're not a competitor, you see? But this bozo . . . Well, never mind. Long as you're sure Lovisi didn't send you.'

Lindsey waved his thanks and slid his key into the lock on his Volvo. Then he stopped and turned back. 'Mr. Anderson! Just a second!'

The big collector turned around. 'Hmm?'

'Do you have this Lovisi fellow's

address? Maybe I should get in touch with him.'

Anderson stood still for a few seconds. Then he said, 'Oh, sure,' and rattled off an address in Brooklyn. Lindsey pulled out his pocket organizer, jotted down the address, and thanked Anderson.

★   ★   ★

At their favorite Italian restaurant in the Richmond Marina, Lindsey and Marvia settled into a comfortable spot in the lounge. It was a cold January night, and outside the lounge's windows the running lights of sailboats sparkled on San Francisco Bay.

After they'd ordered cocktails, Marvia asked Lindsey if he was making any progress finding Albert Crocker Vansittart's beneficiary. Lindsey recounted his paper chase ending in Castro Valley.

Marvia put her hand on Lindsey's. 'It looks as if I'm going to be involved in this case, too.'

'How so?'

'Jamie's video tape's made him a

49

celebrity. CNN made dubs of his tape for editing, but Jamie got his original back. Then the Washoe County Sheriff's Department asked if they could get a look at the tape, and of course my good little citizen was happy to cooperate with law enforcement.'

'I'll bet he was having the time of his life.'

'Well, they got the Coast Guard into the act and studied some of the landmarks and decided that the helicopter crashed in Nevada. Turns out that initial jurisdiction is federal. Airspace is federal, especially on an interstate flight. So it may wind up in California, it may wind up in Nevada. For the moment, Nevada has it.'

Their drinks arrived. Marvia sipped at her hot toddy, then lowered it to the tabletop. 'They're trying to get that fiber-optic scanner down to the chopper. If they do, they're going to need a top computer graphics analyst to help them with it. They've already called one in to try and sharpen up Jamie's tape. See if they can get an image inside the copter bubble before it hit the water. One guess who the designated genius is.'

'Fabia Rabinowitz?'

'Bingo! Your old friend from Cal, right here in town. And guess who's the designated liaison officer between all of these entities.'

'That's great. It means we can talk about this project, feed each other information ... How did you fall into that job?'

Marvia laughed. 'The phone rings at McKinley Avenue this morning and it's a sergeant from the Washoe County Sheriff's Department calling to set up liaison with BPD. The voice I hear sounds strangely familiar. Turns out it's Willie Fergus.'

'I wouldn't know.'

'We were in the army together. We were MPs in Wiesbaden and dated a couple of times, before I got mixed up with the wonderful Lieutenant Wilkerson. I wound up pregnant, then married, then discharged, then divorced, then back in school, then a cop.'

'Ah yes, I remember it well.'

'Willie joined up young, did his twenty and out, and now he's US Army retired and a sergeant for the Washoe County Sheriff. And you know what?'

Lindsey didn't know what.

'Willie thinks there's something fishy about this whole case.'

4

Lindsey watched Chicago grow through the window of a 757. He felt better about the Vansittart case knowing that Marvia Plum was involved in it at the California end, and he felt good about leaving Mother in the capable hands of Gordon Sloane.

She'd been robbed of her husband at the age of seventeen by a tragedy at sea off the coast of North Korea, and spent the better part of forty years in a mental fog, devoting what little sense of reality she'd retained to raising the son her husband never lived to see. It was only when Lindsey started, ever so cautiously, to untie the apron strings and move away from her that Mother began to discover herself. She was not yet sixty. There was still time for her to have a life.

Lindsey recognized the Sears Tower, then Lake Michigan, the pale sun of a late winter's afternoon glinting from its surface.

Before leaving California, he had posted a message on International Surety's KlameNet/Plus system, addressed to his friend and onetime roommate Cletus Berry, now a SPUDS agent in New York. The message included a sketchy rundown on the Vansittart case and the information Lindsey had got from Scotty Anderson. He asked Berry to check on Lovisi in Brooklyn and see what light he could shed on the matter, especially regarding the inquiry Lovisi had received about Paige Publications.

The Boeing touched down and rolled to a stop at Chicago's O'Hare airport.

Lindsey had phoned the SPUDS rep in Chicago, Gina Rossellini. They'd never met, and he wondered what she was like. Her name conjured up the image of a glamorous Italian actress, surely a cross between Gina Lollobrigida and Sophia Loren.

Lindsey had Scotty Anderson's Paige Publications bibliography in his pocket. It was also in his computer and in the electronic case file he'd transmitted to SPUDS headquarters in Denver. Whatever happened to him on this case, the information was safe.

When Lindsey came through the gate he spotted a woman holding a placard with a picture of a potato on it, identical to the one on his lapel. That was the SPUDS logo. She looked like an Italian actress, all right, but not like Lollobrigida or Loren. She looked more like Anna Magnani, *Rose Tattoo* vintage. Definitely the earth-mother type, fleshy and muscular, with olive skin and deep, dark eyes. She wore a black suit, high-heel shoes and big hair.

Gina Rossellini's dark eyes caught sight of Lindsey's lapel pin and she held out her arms like an ideal Mediterranean mother. She had rented a car in Lindsey's name, a white Ford LTD. It was waiting in the airport parking structure.

Lindsey tossed his carry-on luggage and palmtop computer in the Ford's trunk. He'd never been in Chicago before, so Gina drove. Heading away from O'Hare, she told him that she'd heard from Denver. 'You've got a great little job there. All you have to do is track down a model from a forty-year-old painting.'

'Better than that,' Lindsey replied. 'I don't have a copy of the painting. Looks like nobody does.' He told her about his visit to Scotty Anderson. 'At least I wound up with Paige Publications' address. And a list of their books. It's a start.'

'You bet. You busy for dinner?'

The winter darkness had settled quickly over Chicago while he was still in the airport. He could use a good meal and a good rest.

He checked into the Drake Hotel on Lake Shore Drive. It was an elegant establishment; entering the lobby was like stepping into Chicago's past. He half-expected to see Elliot Ness conferring with an underling, or Frank Nitti stubbing out a cigarette in a potted palm.

They gave him a high corner room with windows on two sides and a view of Lake Michigan. There was a lock-bar in one corner, a couple of easy chairs, and an elegant writing desk with a wooden chair. Gina Rossellini said she had some errands to run, and she'd meet him in the Cape Cod Room at 8:00. She'd already made a reservation for them.

Lindsey showered, then phoned Marvia at home, but he'd forgotten the difference in time zones and got only her machine. He told her that he loved her and would talk with her soon. He left his hotel number in case she felt like calling him back, then called his own home and left a similar message for Mother.

Turning on his palmtop computer, he plugged into the hotel's phone line and tapped into KlameNet/Plus. The computer whizzes had enhanced KlameNet into a corporate information system. If you had the right passwords you could tap into International Surety's main data base and file reports, and dredge up records.

Lindsey and all the other SPUDS operatives in the company were told to stand by for a meeting in Denver. The alert contained a little information on the planned program. It looked like a combination pep talk/threat, standard Ducky Richelieu stuff. Lindsey figured there would be a good deal of maneuvering, some promotions announced, and some involuntary transfers posted.

There was nothing new on the Vansittart case. Lindsey had keyed the Paige Publications bibliography into the computer, and even though he still had his paper copy, he called the document up on the screen instead and sat there, staring at the titles and by-lines. *Baseball Stars of 1952*. Was Joe DiMaggio still playing in 1952? Well, no matter. That wasn't likely to have any bearing on the case.

He checked his watch. He'd reset it for Chicago time, and it was nearly time to meet Gina Rossellini at the Cape Cod Room in the hotel. He shut down the computer, pulled on his shoes and slipped into his jacket.

As he was leaving his room, the telephone rang. It was Marvia. She'd heard from Willie Fergus in Reno. The UNR prof had lowered his fiber-optic scanner into Lake Tahoe, looking for the wreckage of Albert Crocker Vansittart's helicopter, and it had located the wreck. At that depth, of course, there was no natural light, but the coaxial fiber-optic cable that could bring back an image to the surface could carry light down to the lake bed. The image, Marvia told Lindsey, was dark and unclear, but there was an image. They were going to bring in a stronger light source and a more sensitive probe and try to get a clearer picture of the crash. Later, Fergus had told Marvia, they hoped to bring up the wreckage, with Albert Crocker Vansittart inside. If he was still there. If something — crabs, fish, or maybe Tahoe Tessie — hadn't eaten him by then.

Lindsey said there was no progress yet, but he was going to work in the morning and he had his hopes.

Marvia said, 'Bart, I miss you. I love you.'

He said, 'Me too.'

Downstairs, the Cape Cod Room was jammed. What Cape Cod had to do with a Chicago hotel was baffling, but the place was attractive and comfortable.

Gina Rossellini must live nearby. Either that, or she kept a change of clothes handy wherever she went, like Clark Kent. The earth-mother look was gone; she actually looked elegant.

The food was good, and Lindsey and Gina Rossellini shared a bottle of Bardolino with it. A brandy afterwards helped, too, and Lindsey was asleep almost before his head hit the pillow.

In the morning Lindsey set out on his quest. The temperature had dropped overnight, and he stopped to buy a hat and a pair of gloves. Maneuvering the white LTD through crowded, slush-choked streets, he found LaSalle and Kinzie, parked, and walked to the site of the Paige Building. He'd expected to find a modest, old-fashioned commercial structure, but instead he found himself gazing at a modern office building that managed to shimmer in the gray mist like the ghost of technology. Surely this was not the Paige Building, but he pushed through revolving doors into the lobby and looked for a building directory, just to be certain.

No, this was not the Paige Building. A uniformed major domo asked if he could help and Lindsey asked if he had ever heard of the Paige Building or of Paige Publications. The man shook his head.

Lindsey started back toward the revolving door, then stopped at the lobby news-stand. The proprietor, sitting behind stacks of Chicago *Tribunes* and *Sun-Times*, looked old enough to remember the first Mayor Daley, if not the earlier lords of the city. Lindsey picked up both morning papers and dropped a bill on the counter. 'You remember the Paige Building?'

The white-haired man looked up at him. 'Sure, I worked there.

'What happened?'

The man shrugged heavy shoulders and grinned. 'They tore it down.'

'When was it torn down? The Paige Building.'

'I know what you mean. That was in, let's see ... ' The man had taken Lindsey's bill but had not bothered to return any change. Lindsey waited.

'This building went up in '88. The

place was a vacant lot in between, you know? Part of the time it was just boarded up; part of the time they let kids play ball here. For a while they had a parking lot here. I worked here all the time. I used to stand on the street hawking papers. I guess you could say I'm the last of the old-time newsboys. They tore down the old place in . . . ' A faraway look came into the old man's eyes. ' . . . in '72. They were going to put up townhouses, but that fell through, so it just stood here for sixteen years. This building now, it's all modern-like, and they have air-conditioning and fancy elevators every place.'

Lindsey said, 'It must be a nice place to work.'

'It stinks. Gimme back the old place any day. People stopped and gave you the time of day. The streets were still safe. Gimme back the old times, any day.'

'What happened to Paige Publications? Were they here until, when was it, '72?'

The old man cackled. 'Old Paige Publications went belly-up back in the early fifties. Oh, they had government men around here then, people coming and going; you'd of thought Joe Staleen personally was running the place. Hell, no, Paige Publications has been gone since Ike was president.'

'Did you know any of the people who worked there?'

The old man reared back in his chair. 'Of course I did. I told you, people had time to give you the time of day back then.'

'Was there actually a Mr. Paige? Did you know him?'

'I used to see him every day, Mr. Paige. He ran the company; had a sweet little wife who used to work there, too. Had a couple of kids. Hey, it broke the old man's heart when he lost that company. He kept the building for a few years, just rented out commercial space; but then he lost that, too. I don't know what happened to him. He's gotta be dead by now. Just like that other poor sap who was takin' flying lessons.'

Lindsey blinked. 'I don't follow.'

'You wouldn't want to.' The old man cackled. 'I mean, flying lessons without no airplane. That poor fella took a header off the roof. I seen him with my own eyes. Was right around the time those gov'ment fellas come around, right around the time Mr. Paige decided to close up the company. One fella used to hang around here all the time; wrote one of them little books for Paige. Went right off the roof.'

'You know that? You saw it?'

'Hell, yes, I seen it. Went across the street for a pack of cigs. I useta sell a lot of them; nobody smokes no more. Back then, ran through a couple cartons a day. But I run out and I wanted a pack for myself. I run across the street to buy a pack of cigs and I turn around and start back and this fella's on the edge of the roof. I seen him. Mr. Paige was up there, tryin' to get him to come back in, but he wouldn't. Went off like a high-diver. Wasn't but five stories, but that was enough. Kilt hisself.'

Lindsey asked, 'Are you sure about this?'

'I had to go testify at the inquest. Man, it was just like bein' on *Perry Mason*. They decided it was an accident — he was up there sunning himself, got dizzy from the sun and fell over the edge. That was that. That was the end of him.'

'What was the man's name?'

'I hardly knew the fella before he tried to fly, then I found his name. Never forget it, neither. Everybody was saying, 'Poor Del, poor Del.' Like, he wrote things, said his name was Del Marston. But at the inquest they said that wasn't his name. I won't forget that, not as long's I live. His real name, they said, was Isidore Horvitz. They said he got dizzy in the sun and fell off the roof, but I know he jumped.'

The old man seemed certain of himself, but Lindsey pressed him. 'How can you be certain that he didn't get dizzy from the sun?'

'I remember that day. It was springtime and it was cold and raining. He wasn't up there for the sun!'

Lindsey switched to another tack. 'Did you know Mr. Paige's first name? Or his wife's or children's?'

The old man rubbed his eyes. 'I think it was Wilbur, William, something like that. I never knew the wife's name, and the kids was just babies.'

Lindsey leaned over the counter. 'Do you know where the Paiges lived?'

'I think somewhere on the north side. Maybe out of town, up in Evanston or Skokie. Plain people could live there back then. You didn't have to be a millionaire to live anyplace. I tell you, mister, the modern world stinks.'

* * *

Lindsey took a light meal, then returned to the Drake. There was an I.S. office in Chicago, and a separate SPUDS operation run by Gina Rossellini, but Lindsey set up a base of operations in his hotel room.

He started with a stack of Chicago-area telephone books. There must be hundreds of Paiges in the greater Chicago area, but the last of the old-time newsboys had mentioned Evanston and Skokie, and that was a logical place to start. Even if Paige, Wilbur or Paige, William, was dead, maybe there was a Wilbur or William Paige, Jr. living in the old house, or at least in the old neighborhood. In the old town. If he couldn't find Paige, he could look for Violet de la Yema or Salvatore Pescara or Del Marston or Walter Roberts or J.B. Harkins or Bob Walters. Somebody still had to be alive. Lindsey would find the survivor.

An hour after starting, he realized that it was mid-afternoon and he hadn't eaten any lunch. He ordered a sandwich and a pot of coffee from room service and went back to work.

After another hour he rolled the room service cart back into the hall, yawned and stretched, and stood at his window looking out over Lake Michigan. Then he went back to work. He'd already tracked down two William Paiges in Skokie as well as three in Evanston, plus three Wilbur Paiges in Skokie, but none in Evanston. Worse, none of the Williams or Wilburs or their spouses or children had anything to do with Paige Publications, or had even heard of Paige Publications.

Lindsey took the elevator downstairs, walked into the bar, and ordered a whiskey. There was a TV set above the back bar tuned to CNN. Of course there was a set in Lindsey's room, but he hadn't turned it on. The announcer intoned, 'These are the photographs that have the world of ichthyology in an uproar. Have scientists from the University of Nevada really found Tahoe Tessie, the mountain lake's cousin of Scotland's famous Loch Ness Monster? Or is it merely a sunken log, or perhaps an overgrown Mackinaw trout?' The image cut to a perfect co-anchor team seated behind a news desk.

The bartender used the remote control to cut the volume on the set. 'Lake Tahoe, hey? That's a little puddle. Those professors ought to take a look at the bottom of Lake Michigan. Then they'd see what a real monster looks like. Waddaya think?'

Lindsey said, 'You're absolutely right.' He paid for his whiskey, left most of it in its glass, and headed back to his room. Once there, he looked out the window again at the now-black sky and black lake. He sighed and went back to work. Should he keep trying Paiges in Evanston and

Skokie, but not limit himself to William or Wilbur? He decided to try.

Another hour's work and he hit paydirt. He'd had to go a little past Evanston, but not very far. A Paul Paige on Willow Road in Winnetka announced that he'd just got home from work at the Chicago Museum of Science and Industry, where he was a senior curator. Yes, he knew about Paige Publications and the Paige Building. No, he didn't know any William or Wilbur Paige, but his father had been Walter Paige, founder and president of Paige Publications. No, he was no longer alive. Nor was his wife, alas. But Paul was alive and well, thank you very much, and what was it that Mr. Lindsey wanted? Lindsey explained that he was with International Surety and was trying to find the beneficiary of a life insurance policy.

Mr. Paige said, 'I've heard 'em all, brother, and believe me, that one's the oldest in the book.'

Lindsey dialed Winnetka again. This time a woman answered. Lindsey asked, 'Is this Mrs. Paul Paige? I'm trying to — '

'I'm his sister. Are you the insurance man?'

'Yes, but I'm not a salesman. I give you my word of honor.'

'Then just what do you want?'

Lindsey tried to explain the Vansittart situation in twenty-five words or less. He must have done pretty well, because the woman finally said, 'All right, you may come to the house. Tonight. It's almost six-thirty now. We should finish our dinner by eight o'clock. You may join us then for coffee. Paul and I will try to assist you.' Lindsey thanked her. 'But I warn you,' she added, 'if you even try to sell me anything, I will go in the other room and get my gun and come back and kill you. I'm not joking.' She hung up.

The phone rang. It was Gina Rossellini. Did he need any help with the case, and was he looking for company for dinner? He thanked her for the offer but begged off.

He dialed Marvia at Berkeley police headquarters. He got through to her and told her that he'd located the Paige family and was going out to their house in an hour. She said that Willie Fergus had called and told her that the fiber-optic probe at Lake Tahoe was getting good results. Lindsey told her about his conversation with the bartender. They promised to keep each other informed.

★ ★ ★

The Paige home on Willow Road was a tall Tudor set behind a broad lawn. A gravel drive led to the front door. Lindsey's prospective hosts had left a light burning — that was a good sign. The house sported a three-car garage, but there was already a new-looking Chevy Caprice in the driveway. Maybe there was more company tonight, or maybe the Paiges were a four-car family.

The woman who answered the door wore a black maid's uniform complete with white apron and cap. She took his fedora and topcoat and his card away and came back and ushered him into the living room.

Yes indeed, the family was assembled for their after-dinner coffee, and Lindsey

71

was invited to join the fun. The woman who rose to greet him wore her white hair in a graceful upsweep that might not have been current but was definitely fashionable. She wore a dark green woolen dress and a simple golden chain that reached halfway down her chest. A tiny golden crucifix hung from the chain. Jesus looked happy and contented between the woman's breasts. She had received Lindsey's card and glanced at it as he approached.

She shook his hand. He noticed a wedding band and a large glittering rock. 'I am Patti Paige Hanson. You are Mr. Lindsey. Please sit down. Doreen will bring you a cup of coffee. Or would you prefer tea?'

'Coffee would be just fine.'

She steered him to a sofa. Doreen poured the coffee. The silver was polished and the china, Lindsey would have bet, did not come from Japan. Tiny cubes of sugar were served with tiny silver tongs formed into tiny birds' claws.

There were three more people in the room. The older man — his features faintly resembled Patti Paige Hanson's

— sat quietly observing. His hair was not pure white, like Patti Paige Hanson's; it was silvery gray. His face was seamed and leathered, with the look of an outdoorsman's. He wore a blue pinstripe suit, a white shirt, and quiet tie. He nodded to Lindsey and said, 'I'm Paul Paige. We spoke on the phone.'

A boy who might be a youthful twenty or a regular sixteen sat on the edge of an easy chair. He wore a hound's-tooth jacket, a button-down shirt, striped tie, and flannel slacks. A girl who might be a year or two younger sat sideways in another easy chair. Her hair was cropped boyishly short and dyed jet black. She wore death-white makeup, black eyeliner and black lipstick. Her clothing was black and ripped in three or four places. She wore one fingerless glove.

Paul Paige said, 'Ah, my nephew, Theo, and my niece, Selena. Hanson. Theo and Selena Hanson. They're my sister's children by her late husband, Gelett. Gelett Burgess Hanson, a nephew of the original Gelett Burgess. You've heard of Gelett Burgess, the famous author?'

Theo Hanson stood up and advanced to Lindsey. Lindsey stood. The boy said, 'A pleasure to meet you, sir.' He shook hands with Lindsey, then returned to his seat. Selena Hanson sneered at Lindsey.

Lindsey confessed that he had never heard of Gelett Burgess, the famous author.

Patti Paige Hanson said, 'A pity. His books are worthy of attention. I suggest that you investigate them when you return to your home.' She paused to preen briefly, then went on, 'Now, Mr. Lindsey, just what was it about this alleged insurance policy? My father — Paul's and mine — was indeed in the publishing business in the early 1950s. But you were not very clear on the telephone about this insurance policy.'

Lindsey went over the case again. Mrs. Hanson seemed to listen intently. Lindsey couldn't be sure about the rest of the family. 'What I was hoping, then, was to find any kind of records of Paige Publications. Personnel files, financial records, anything that could help me find the woman on the cover of *Death in the Ditch*.'

Mrs. Hanson shook her head. 'Father seldom spoke of the publishing business. That all ended so long ago, then he concentrated on real estate. He had hard going for several years, but eventually he did very well, as you can see.' Her gesture included the room, but it seemed to indicate the whole house, maybe all of Winnetka.

'There's a new building on the old Paige site at LaSalle and Kinzie,' Lindsey said.

'Yes.'

'I was there today and spoke with the man who runs the news kiosk in the lobby. He says he knew your father and mother. Knew both of you when you were small children.'

Mrs. Hanson shot a look at her brother. 'I wouldn't remember any of that. I was just a baby. So was Paul.'

'The thing is, he mentioned some government agents visiting your father. Said that they came around repeatedly.'

'Probably about taxes. Or some bureaucratic matter. They're a pack of self-serving socialists in Washington. If not worse. Let me tell you something — the Soviet Union was never a threat to this country. The communist menace comes from Washington, not from Russia. From Washington and Boston and Jew York. Decent people are going to have to build walls around themselves soon to keep the other kind out.'

That's what Lindsey thought she said. He didn't ask her to repeat it. He said, 'I do have a list of books that Paige Publications issued.' He unfolded Scotty Anderson's printout and spread it on the coffee table. Theo Hanson came over and looked at it. Selena Hanson sneered.

Patti Paige Hanson said, 'I'm sure I am not interested. What I would really like to know, Mr. Lindsey, is whether this insurance settlement involved the Paige family. If this money was left to an employee, perhaps the company is entitled to the money. I mean, some casual model, not even an employee, really. I never met Mr. Vansittart, but of course I knew of him. I was shocked to hear of his death. I'd think that the money should come to the company, you know, under the law of agency.'

Lindsey shook his head. 'I doubt that, frankly. It's really a question for Legal, of course, but I really don't think so.'

Mrs. Hanson reached into a purse that appeared miraculously and extracted a jeweled eyeglass case. She unfolded a small pair of glasses and perched them on her nose. Lindsey almost expected her to use a lorgnette. She peered at the Anderson bibliography and sniffed, then shook her head. 'No. No.' She shoved the paper back toward Lindsey.

'Do you think your father might have left any personal notes on the company? Correspondence? If I could just get a lead on this woman . . . '

'Nothing.' Mrs. Hanson stood up. Her brother and son followed suit. Selena swung one leg over the end of her chair, up and down and up and down.

Doreen reappeared with Lindsey's hat and coat. She must have been summoned telepathically. She helped Lindsey into the coat and handed him the hat. He turned to Mrs. Hanson and the others. 'If you do think of anything, I'll be at the Drake for a little longer. Or you could try me at International Surety in Chicago after that; they'll get the message to me. If you do think of anything.'

Paul Paige and Theo Hanson shook his hand. Patti Paige Hanson sniffed, touched her fingertips to his, and turned back into the house. Paul Paige wished Lindsey a safe drive back to Chicago.

5

Not long after Lindsey arrived back at his hotel, his phone rang. 'This is Sarah Kleinhoffer.' The voice was low, almost a whisper.

'I'm sorry, I can hardly hear you, Miss — '

'Then listen harder, stupid. I have to keep my voice down. I don't want her to hear me.'

Lindsey was annoyed. 'I think you have the wrong room.'

'You're Lindsey the insurance man. You were just at my house. What's your room number? I have to see you, OK? I'm going to sneak out of here. Just don't leave, all right? Just stay put. What's your room number?' He told her. She hung up.

Lindsey turned on the TV and channel-surfed. He finally settled on a rerun of a black-and-white episode of *Bewitched*. He must have dozed, because he was awakened by a soft tapping at his door. Stumbling across the room in his suit trousers, shirt, and socks, he opened the door and confronted a witch — black hair, pale skin, black lips, black tattered clothes. She was clutching a shapeless sack that might contain anything from a jack-o'-lantern to a flock of vampire bats.

'That thug in the comic-opera uniform didn't want to let me in,' she snarled. 'Good thing Theo was along. My goody-goody brother.'

Lindsey's head was beginning to clear. The witch was Selena Hanson. Selena, not Serena, but close enough. Her tweed-jacketed brother Theo stood behind her, grinning uncertainly.

'Uh — come in. I thought your name was Paige. Why did you say you were Sarah Kleinhoffer?'

The two young people moved past Lindsey, Sarah/Selena brusquely, Theo diffidently. As if he'd never left Winnetka, Theo perched carefully on the edge of a chair. His sister flung herself on the bed. She plopped her witch's sack beside her hip.

'My real name is Kleinhoffer.' She

looked around. 'Great pad. You got any dope?'

Lindsey gawked.

'Never mind. The bitch's real name is Kleinhoffer, too. Was. I guess she came by the Hanson honestly; she did marry the guy. But I wouldn't want the same name as her, so I went back to Kleinhoffer.'

What was this all about? Lindsey decided to take it bit by bit. 'You're talking about your mother, of course.'

'*Duhhh*, no kidding.'

'Her maiden name was Paige. Her father was Walter Paige, of Paige Publications. Her brother is Paul Paige, right? And your mother was Patti Paige? Like the singer?'

'I wouldn't know.'

'Patti Page was a very popular singer at one time. She spelled it differently but it sounds the same.'

'I wouldn't know.' Sarah/Selena pushed herself upright on the bed. She reached for the remote, turned on the TV, hit the mute button and surfed until she came to a shopping channel. 'Look,' she said, 'I don't know what this business is all

81

about, but I hate that bitch with her social climbing and her fancy airs. She's an uptight, materialistic bigot. She's a racist and an anti-Semite. That's why I took back Grandpa's name. Kleinhoffer.'

'You . . . ' Lindsey looked from Sarah to Theo. Theo nodded silently. Lindsey looked back at Sarah. 'Walter Paige wasn't his real name?'

'Grandpa changed his name for business. Assimilation, that was what they all wanted to do back then. In his personal life he was still Kleinhoffer. And his first name wasn't Walter, it was Werner. He was a German Jew who got out of Europe just in the nick of time. Hitler and all that, you know.'

'Yes, I do.' Lindsey nodded.

'He came to America and assimilated. I don't think it was right, but I can't blame him either. Not after what he'd seen in Europe.'

'Aren't you awfully young to know all this?' Lindsey asked.

'I'm fifteen.'

'Is that why your brother came along?' He nodded to Theo.

'Theo drove the Caprice. I would have driven myself, but the last time I got busted driving without a license they kept me overnight in jail and the bitch threatened to send me to boarding school if I got busted again.'

Lindsey looked at Theo. 'Is this all true? I mean, do you agree with your sister?'

Theo nodded. 'Every word, sir.'

Sarah laughed. 'Theo's the radical in the family. I'm just a mild case compared to him. The straight clothes and the polite manners are just protective coloration. I guess he's right, but I couldn't make myself wear those stupid clothes and go to her stupid luncheons and mix with her stupid, shallow, bitchy friends. But hey, Theo puts me in the shade.'

'Is that true, Theo?' Lindsey asked.

'Yes, sir,' the young man said.

Sarah burst into laughter. 'If you don't have any dope, a shot of booze would do.'

'Uh, I don't know. I mean, that would be illegal.'

'Right. Go take a leak while I open that little lock-bar. What's the combination? Don't tell me, just hold up your fingers.'

Lindsey gave her the combination.

She opened the lock-bar, tossed a miniature Scotch to her brother, and took one for herself. 'Nothing for you, Mr. Lindsey?'

'Uh, I don't think so.'

Sarah shrugged, twisted the top off the bottle, and raised it high. 'Here's looking at you, kid.' She drained the miniature in one swig. At least she had good taste in movies.

Lindsey went to the writing desk and sat down. 'You know that I'm looking for a model, right? You heard me explain things to your mother and your uncle? His name is really Paul Paige, isn't it?'

'Paul Paige or Paul Kleinhoffer, take your pick.'

'How old were you when your grandfather died? Had he told you all this — about escaping Hitler and changing his name, I mean?'

Theo took over the dialog. 'I was thirteen and Sarah was ten. Dad had already died, and Mother refused to go to Granddad's funeral. The Jewish Sacred Society did the burying. The Jewish community honored him. The funeral procession passed the Mishna Ugmoro Synagogue on the way to the cemetery, and they opened the doors of the temple. I don't know if you understand that, Mr. Lindsey. Somebody not Jewish might not understand. We don't bring the dead into the synagogue. But to open the doors as the procession passes means a great deal.'

Theo paused to gather his thoughts, then he continued. 'He was buried at the Shalom Memorial Park out in Palatine. He'd left instructions in his will; he'd talked with his lawyer about it, and if Mother changed his instructions she would have lost her inheritance. She was furious. She said she might have gone to the service if it hadn't been Orthodox. She just couldn't put up with people tearing their clothes in grief, not washing, covering mirrors. She called it all absurd, throwback superstition. She couldn't see how her father would do such a thing to her.'

Sarah interrupted with a giggle, then Theo resumed his narration. 'She left town. She wanted us all to leave town and boycott the funeral, can you believe that? But Uncle Paul insisted on staying and Sarah and I stayed with him. Mother didn't get over it for months. She still beats us up with it when we get her riled.'

'And he was buried as Kleinhoffer?' Lindsey asked. 'Werner Kleinhoffer?'

'That's right. Of course Sarah and I were baffled by the whole thing. We thought he was Walter Paige. We thought Mother was Patti Paige Hanson, not Patti Kleinhoffer Hanson. So after the funeral, Uncle Paul took us out for dinner at Charlie Trotter's over by Halstead. He let us order cocktails. The waiter was pretty miffed, but Uncle Paul was a regular there and he got away with it. And he told us everything.'

'Why are you telling me this? Why did you come here?'

Sarah rummaged in her witch's pack and emerged with a hand mirror and lipstick. She proceeded to replenish the blackness of her lips. Around the lipstick she answered Lindsey's question.

'To burn the bitch.'

'Theo,' Lindsey said, nodding, 'you feel

the same way? But you seem to be going along with your mother's game plan, her whole lifestyle.'

Theo grinned. 'This will get me into any college I want. This is my junior year at prep school and I've already been accepted at Northwestern, University of Chicago, Oberlin, Harvard, Brown, Princeton, and Yale. I might have preferred McGill or Cambridge, or maybe the Sorbonne, but Mom thinks that any college outside the US would just fill my head with bad thoughts.' He laughed.

'You say your uncle told you all this family history.'

'Right.'

'What's his role in the household? If your mother is as bad as you say, why does he live with you? Is he a widower? Divorced? Or what?'

'He was never married.' Theo had got a glass from the bathroom, some ice cubes from the bar, and built himself a Scotch-on-the-rocks. 'Some story about a grand love, tragedy, heartbreak. Melodramatic stuff, Aaron Spelling. Danielle Steele kind of stuff. He's lived with us as long as I can remember.'

He took a careful sip of his Scotch-on-the-rocks. Sarah climbed off the bed and took another bottle from the lock bar. Theo leaned back in his chair. 'Uncle Paul is a good-hearted wuss. He hangs out with Sarah and me. He knows what Mom is, but he won't confront her.' He paused, then added, 'Do you think you'll really find this model?'

'I really don't know. The name Werner Kleinhoffer might be of help. It would have helped a lot more if he were still alive. Are there any other surviving relatives other than your mom and your uncle?'

'Nobody.' Sarah took careful aim and tossed an empty miniature into the waste basket beside the desk. She held the second empty over her mouth, coaxing a drop of Scotch from the bottle. 'Adolf got 'em all. He really didn't like us Jews, you know.'

Lindsey caught an exchanged nod between Sarah and Theo. Sarah got off the bed and carried her witch's pack to Lindsey's desk. 'Grandpa kept a lot of records. All his life. When the Paige Building was gone, he brought them home. He wouldn't throw anything away. Uncle Paul says that Grandpa always felt that Paige Publications should have been a success; that it was ruined by those fascist bastards from Washington. Uncle Paul says that Grandpa wanted to keep an archive so that the family would see someday that he was doing something fine with Paige Publications.'

Lindsey nodded. Sarah resumed, 'Then when Grandpa died, Uncle Paul says, the bitch burned everything.'

Lindsey waited.

'But Uncle Paul saved something.' She opened her witch's pack and reached inside. Carefully, one by one, she removed the nine objects it contained and laid them out in neat formation on Lindsey's desk. They were a complete mint set of Paige Publications books, including both the *Teen Gangs of Chicago* and the *Al Capone's Heirs* versions of Paige serial number 104/105.

Theo Hanson stood next to his sister. He put his tweed-coated arm around her shoulders and she slid her slim arm in its ragged black sleeve around his waist. Theo laid his free hand on Lindsey's shoulder.

'We want you to take the books, Mr. Lindsey. We even talked this over with Uncle Paul. He was afraid to come with us; he was afraid that Mom might wake up and think the house was too quiet and start looking for us, and then the *merde* would really hit the fan. So he stayed home in Winnetka to calm her down if she starts to make a fuss. But he wants you to take the books, too. He's afraid that Mom will find them in his room and take them out and burn them, and that will be the end of Grandpa's dream.'

Lindsey could have sworn that there were tears in Theo's eyes. 'We want you to take them, Mr. Lindsey, and see to it that they're safe. Maybe they should be donated to a library or something, but we were afraid that Mother would find a way to get them back and destroy them. Don't let her do that, Mr. Lindsey. Promise you'll take care of the books.'

Lindsey promised. Then he asked, 'Do

either of you know anything about Del Marston?'

Theo pointed to the books. 'I know his novel. That's all.'

'About his death?' Lindsey asked.

Theo shook his head, no. Lindsey looked at Sarah. No.

'Or Isidore Horvitz?'

'*Nada*. Blank. Sorry. Who's Isidore Horvitz?'

'I think he was Del Marston,' Lindsey replied. 'I think he killed himself sometime in the early 1950s. Long before your time. I just thought that your uncle might have said something about him.'

'Sorry.' Then, 'About the books . . . '

Lindsey promised to guard them, to make sure they found a good home.

Theo and Sarah seemed satisfied. Theo said, 'Thanks, Mr. Lindsey. You do what you can. I don't think you should try to contact us. Just take the books and find that woman. I think Grandpa would be pleased.'

The two youngsters headed for the door. Before they left, Theo said, 'Thanks again, Mr. Lindsey.'

Sarah said, 'Thanks for the booze. Some hop would have been better, but the booze was okay.'

Lindsey blinked. The youngsters were already in the hallway, but he stepped out and called them back. 'I'm sorry. I just — what about this Burgess fellow your mother mentioned? He'd be, I guess, some kind of second or third cousin of yours. Your parents seem to think he was important. Do you — ?'

'We have his books at home,' Theo supplied. 'Mother keeps them in a place of honor. They were just murder mysteries. Of course Mother refers to them as criminological studies. They're in a glass bookcase under lock and key.'

Theo and Sarah started toward the elevator, then Sarah stopped her brother again. 'Nobody reads old Cousin Gelett's books any more. But I'll bet you've heard his *magnum opus*.'

'I have?'

'*I've never seen a purple cow*,' Sarah quoted.

'*I never hope to see one*,' Theo continued.

'*But this I know and know full well,*' they chanted in unison, '*I'd rather see than be one.*'

Theo took his sister by the hand and they left.

Lindsey returned to the desk and laid out the Paige Publications books again. Typical paperbacks of their era, with garish colors and lurid blurbs. But for all that, they looked like brand-new books. Out of curiosity, he picked up the beautiful copy of *Buccaneer Blades* and opened it, ever so carefully, to the title page. In blue-black ink that had not faded with the years, someone had written *Salud y Suerte, Violeta*. He had never seen the inscription in Scotty Anderson's *Buccaneer Blades*, so he could not tell if the handwriting was the same.

Lindsey got into his pajamas and climbed into bed. He left the drapes pulled back, the room lights off, and watched the first large snowflakes of a new storm drift by his window, illuminated by the lurid colors of an advertising sign.

★　★　★

The bright morning sun warmed Lindsey's face and woke him. He ordered breakfast from room service, then set up his palmtop and logged into KlameNet/ Plus while he waited for the cart to arrive. There was a message from SPUDS/ Denver. The World Fund for Indigent Artists had filed for Albert Crocker Vansittart's death benefits. The claim had reached Desmond Richelieu and he had personally started the Standard Corporate Delay Hourglass running. Lindsey was to contact the Cookes in San Francisco a.s.a.p.

It was too early to phone anyone in California, including Marvia Plum, so he turned to his meal. Both Chicago morning papers, the *Trib* and the *Sun-Times*, were included with Lindsey's order from room service. He browsed through the newspapers while he ate his scrambled eggs and sweet pastries.

He turned to the sports section. There was the standard hype that preceded the Super Bowl each January, but with the

Bears out of the running as usual, the local sheets were more interested in the ongoing exploits of the Chicago Bulls.

Lindsey put down the newspapers and picked up his coffee. Something was tickling inside his skull. He squeezed his eyes shut trying to bring it into focus. An image appeared in his mind, something that had happened only a few hours ago. Sarah Kleinhoffer in her stark black outfit, emptying her witch's pack onto his desk, spreading the nine books that Paige Publications had issued during its brief career in 1951 and 1952.

He opened his eyes. The books were still there. He picked up *Baseball Stars of 1952* by J.B. Harkins. Werner Kleinhoffer and, after Kleinhoffer's death, Paul Paige, must have kept the nine books in a safe place for all those years, because the covers were just as bright and glossy as they would be on brand-new books.

Lindsey picked up the baseball book and turned it over. There was no author photo or biography on the back, but then there seldom was on paperbacks. Paperback publishers usually devoted that precious display space to harder-sell material, either for the book at hand or for others in their line. That was what Paige Publications did. The back cover of *Baseball Stars of 1952* featured a miniature reproduction of the cover of *I Was a Lincoln Brigadier* by Bob Walters.

That seemed odd to Lindsey. You'd expect a cross-promotion to be devoted to a book with a similar theme — a western on a western, he thought, or a mystery on a mystery. Of course, Paige had turned out so few books that that might have been impossible.

Lindsey laid the book back down, then turned over the other eight titles. Now an interesting difference revealed itself. On the 1951 titles, the cross-promotion principle was carried out. He'd already seen one Paige book, Scotty Anderson's copy of *Buccaneer Blades*, with promotion material for *Death in the Ditch* on the back cover. Now he held a copy of *Death in the Ditch*, and its back cover ad space was given over to *Cry Ruffian!* by Salvatore Pescara. Okay, he mused, that one made sense. *Cry Ruffian!* was blurbed as 'A rough, tough, angry novel of a poor kid who vowed to make society pay for his father's death — and kept his word!' There were a great many exclamation points on the back covers of Paige Publications books.

The 1951 books worked like a round-robin. *Buccaneer Blades* promoted *Death in the Ditch*, which promoted *Cry Ruffian!*, which promoted *Teen Gangs of Chicago*, which promoted *Buccaneer Blades*. The books were numbered 101 through 104.

But *Al Capone's Heirs* was something different. It was the same book as *Teen Gangs of Chicago*. Lindsey checked the contents of the two books, carefully opening them only as far as he needed to, so the dried glue that held the pages to the cover wouldn't crack. No question about it. Only the cover and the title pages were different. But *Al Capone's Heirs*, Paige number 105, must have come out after the 1952 Paige line was in progress, because its back cover was given over to promoting *I Was a Lincoln Brigadier*. And *all* of the 1952 Paiges had the same back cover: a miniature reproduction of the *Lincoln Brigadier* cover, and an almost poetic paean to the Spanish War volunteers, with a long quotation from Ernest Hemingway, of all people.

More to the point, though, was the copy of the Del Marston book. Lindsey returned to *Death in the Ditch*, studying the gang moll on the cover. 'Schweetheart,' he whispered to himself in his best Bogie imitation, 'you've got one big pile of money coming to you.' And then added, 'If you're still alive. And if I can find you.'

Lindsey stacked the nine Paige books carefully and packed them away in his airplane luggage. He carried the Chicago papers back to the desk and leafed through them again, then he opened his luggage and extracted *Baseball Stars of 1952*. On the front cover, beneath J.B. Harkins' by-line, was the tag, *Ace Chicago Sports Reporter!* Lindsey couldn't figure out why that rated an exclamation point, but who was he to judge?

He checked the Chicago telephone directory for J.B. Harkins. No such listing. He looked up the Chicago *Sun-Times*, punched in a number, and asked for the sports desk. Two minutes later he was talking with Maude Markham. He'd found her picture at the head of a column called 'Fifty Years Ago in Chicagoland Sports,' and from the looks of the photo she was more likely to write from memory than she was from the newspaper's doubtlessly extensive morgue.

Lindsey could have asked his questions on the phone, but he'd found in the past that personal contacts often yielded better results than telephone inquiries. He cut an unprepossessing figure, he knew that, and he was the master of a ploy that he called the *I'm-just-a-poor-working-stiff-doing-my-job-ma'am-won't-you-please-help-me-out* approach.

Maude Markham sounded like an amalgam of Marjorie Main and Jane Darwell — strong, gruff, with just a touch of the old heart-of-gold. She'd just shivered in from covering a Polar Bear Club meeting and swim in Lake Michigan, she announced, and she was freezing her bunions off. If Lindsey wanted to come to the office and ask her a few questions about old-time Chicago sports, she could give him a few minutes. He said he'd be right over.

An hour later he arrived at the *Sun-Times* building. Leaving the Drake, he'd been presented with a spectacular sight — downtown Chicago glistening in bright sunlight under a coat of fresh, sparkling snow. Now he walked through the lobby of the *Sun-Times*, confirmed that he really had an appointment with Maude Markham, and rode up in the elevator to present himself. He had his pocket organizer and his International Surety gold pencil with him, his shield and his lance. And in another pocket, carefully protected by a Hotel Drake envelope, *Baseball Stars of 1952*.

Maude Markham was a perfect match for her voice and for the picture that headed her column in the *Sun-Times*. She had an electric space-heater beside her desk, sending orange-red warmth toward her knees. Her first words to Lindsey were, 'You'd think that five columns a week would be enough for the sonsabitches, but I have to take spot assignments to boot. Damn Polar Bears, they ought to freeze their nuts off in that freezing lake, then I could sleep in every January.' She nodded toward the space heater. 'Illegal as hell. Nobody better try and take it away from me or I'll skin 'em alive.' Then she looked at Lindsey and said, 'What can I do for you, sweetums? I don't have as many swains as I used to.'

'I was wondering if you ever knew J.B. Harkins.'

Maude Markham's eyes popped. 'Jeb Harkins? Of course. Everybody knew Jeb.'

Lindsey started to speak but she cut him off. 'What are you after, bubby? You must be the first person to ask about Jeb in maybe twenty years.'

Lindsey didn't want to go into the whole Vansittart/Paige Publications/*Death in the Ditch* story so he said, 'Harkins wrote a book called *Baseball Stars of 1952*, right?'

Maude Markham nodded. 'I even did a column on it. I write about fiftieth anniversaries, so I did a piece on Jeb's book when spring training opened in '92. Filed from Florida. I hope they have a baseball season this year; I could sure use a little Florida sunshine.'

Lindsey wrinkled his brow. 'Wait a minute. 1992 minus fifty doesn't give us 1952, it gives '42.'

Maude Markham grinned. 'You ain't so dumb, sweetie. Smarter than my editor is; he didn't catch on. I figure by the real fiftieth anniversary, Jeb might not be around anymore to enjoy the piece I wrote. Hades, I might not be around to write it. So what the heck, I went ahead. And you know how many letters I had about it? Not one, would you believe that? Not one. The world is full of morons.'

Lindsey nodded encouragingly.

'I sent Jeb a copy of the piece, and he wrote me back a letter, like to break my heart. Poor old bastard. We used to have some great fights, but he didn't deserve what happened to him.' She shook her head, then turned away from Lindsey and punched up a file on the monitor screen on her desk. Lindsey read the headline. *Polar Bears Brave Snow Storm and Icy Lake for Big Swim*. Maude Markham said, 'They try to rotate that assignment, send somebody else out every year to cover the Polar Bear swim. Doesn't matter. They always come back with the same story. Change a few names to cover the old bears dying off and the young ones joining the club, you could recycle last year's copy.' She blanked the screen and swung around in her swivel chair. 'You have a copy of Jeb's book?'

'Yes.'

'Real nice. So do I. So what?'

'Well, I'm actually trying to track down a woman who modeled for another book published by the same company. The same company that published *Baseball Stars of 1952*, you see, and I thought if Mr. Harkins is still alive, and I could talk with him, he might be able to help me. So if you could help me get in touch with Mr. Harkins, don't you see — '

Maude Markham looked up at Lindsey. 'You really have a copy of that book?

'Cause I haven't seen a copy in eons, ducks, except the one on my shelf at home.'

'Here it is.' Lindsey laid his copy of *Baseball Stars of 1952* on Maude Markham's desk. He grinned.

Maude Markham gingerly opened the Drake Hotel envelope. She must know something about old books, then, or maybe she was just naturally cautious. She slipped the book out of the envelope and laid it on her desk. She smiled wistfully.

'Look at those ballparks.'

The cover of *Baseball Stars of 1952* featured a montage of faces of ballplayers in their colorful caps, and around them, like a giant wreath, a circle of pictures of stadiums. The players' portraits looked like miniature paintings; the ballparks were pen-and-ink sketches. All of this on the cover of a book no bigger than four inches wide and six inches tall. Some of the ballplayers' caps Lindsey recognized, if not the men wearing them. Others might have belonged to the Beijing Ducks for all he could tell.

Tersely, Maude Markham identified the teams for him. You ain't a baseball fan, are you, sweetcakes? No, I didn't think so.'

'And Mr. Harkins himself?'

'What about him? Great old-time news hound. Went way back. Way back. Used to work at the old *Daily News*. Got his jock-journalist start on the *Inter-Ocean*. Bet you never heard of the *Inter-Ocean*, did you?'

Lindsey admitted he had not.

'Terrible paper. But an old news hound could always get a gig there. More alcoholics than a drunk-tank on New Year's morning. But it was a lot of fun. Oh, yes. Old Jeb, he worked with Vincent Starrett, Ben Hecht — he knew everybody; told stories you wouldn't believe. It killed me when he retired. I always felt young when the old coot was around. Nowadays, everybody thinks *I'm* old. *I* even think I'm old. What were you asking me, darling?'

'About J.B. Jeb Harkins. Where he is now? He's still alive, isn't he?'

'Far as I know.'

'Then — ?'

'Jeb was one of those poor souls who keeps falling in love with the wrong woman and getting thrown over, you know what I mean? Got married three or four times. Had a son with one wife; boy was in the air force, got shot down over Russia, never heard of again. Whole thing was hushed up, just one more cold war casualty. Had a daughter; she got married, had some kids. They went off to God-knows-where; Jeb's daughter and her husband moved to San Francisco. Then he died, and she couldn't take it being alone, so she talked Jeb into coming to live with her.'

She shook her head, looking past Lindsey, seeing something that he might see someday. 'Bad move. He lost his place, you know what I mean? New surroundings, new people. He wasn't independent any more, poor old coot. Then his daughter got sick and she couldn't take care of him anymore, so she put him in a home. Then she died. And there he is. I don't know what the hell he does with himself. Probably sits around

106

waiting for the undertaker, poor old coot.'

Lindsey felt for his pocket organizer, slipped it unobtrusively out of his jacket, and revved up his gold pencil. 'Ms. Markham — Maude — did you know anybody else connected with Paige Publications?'

'Nope. Just Jeb, and only because we worked for the same paper.'

'Do you have an address for the nursing home, or a phone number? What kind of shape is he in? Do you think he could answer some questions about Paige?'

Maude Markham laughed. She flipped open an industrial-grade Rolodex and pulled out a card, then laid it on the desk in front of Lindsey. He jotted down the information and put away his pocket organizer and gold pencil.

'One other thing,' Lindsey said. 'Did you ever meet Del Marston? Or Isidore Horvitz?

A new expression came across Maude's face. 'Of course I did. Everybody knew about him.'

'What really happened? How did he die?'

'Got dizzy. What a tragedy. Only man I ever heard of, dying of dizziness. Went up on the roof of the Paige Building to sunbathe and got dizzy from the sun and fell over the parapet. I think he must have been drinking a little, too. Booze will do that to you, booze and strong sunlight.'

Lindsey tilted his head. 'But I thought he died on a rainy day. Cold and rainy.'

Maude said, 'It was the sun. Sun and booze. Look, I'm really a busy person, I have to do my job. If you don't mind.' She pulled her outermost sweater up until her face was half-concealed, then turned away.

Lindsey said, 'Thank you, Ms. Markham. You've been a lot of help.' Then he left the *Sun-Times* building. At least he'd got another lead. He had J.B. Harkins' address. Harkins lived at the Shady Oaks Retirement Villas in Livermore, California.

Lindsey had done about all he could do in Chicago. He retrieved his Ford LTD and drove carefully back to the Drake on Lake Shore. Once upstairs in his room, he packed his belongings and called the desk to have his bill prepared. Before putting his palmtop in its case, he plugged it into a phone line for one more check of KlameNet/Plus.

There was a message waiting for him from Cletus Berry. Berry had located Lovisi at the Brooklyn address Scotty Anderson had given Lindsey. Lovisi had been open and cooperative. He told Berry that the inquiry he'd received shortly before arranging to run Anderson's piece in *Paperback Parade* had surprised him because *Death in the Ditch* and all the Paige books were so very obscure. Even many serious collectors had never heard of Paige Publications. And most of the serious collectors knew each other, either in person or at least by reputation.

Lovisi had never heard of the person looking for information on the Marston book. It was an unusual name, too. Lovisi hadn't written it down; he hadn't needed to. He had an eidetic memory. The caller's name was Nathan ben Zinowicz. The only address ben Zinowicz had given was an electronic mail number. As far as Lovisi — or Cletus Berry — knew, the e-mail could be picked up from anywhere. Just as Lindsey had picked up Berry's message here in Chicago.

Lindsey felt a cold hand grab his insides and squeeze. Nathan ben Zinowicz was the man behind the theft of the rare comic books that had started Lindsey on his career as a de facto detective. Ben Zinowicz might not have killed the poor kid who operated the comic book store, but he was the man who beat a young woman and put her in a wheelchair for life, and he was the man who had put a bullet through Lindsey's foot and left him to drown — very nearly — in San Francisco Bay. And he was the man who — the local police said they had no jurisdiction and the United States Navy didn't want to hear about it — but he was the man, Lindsey was morally certain, who had caused Lindsey's father's death aboard the destroyer *Lewiston* in the Sea of Japan, a few months before Lindsey himself was born.

Lindsey sent a brief thanks to Berry, then he opened the Vansittart file and updated it before logging off. He phoned the airline and reserved a flight back to Oakland. Fortunately the snowfall had ended and O'Hare was open.

Lindsey passed up the food on the 757. By the time it touched down at Oakland International he had a first-rate appetite. He'd splurged International Surety's money to place an in-flight telephone call to Marvia and another to his mother. He told Mother he was on his way home and he'd see her either late tonight or else tomorrow. She was pleased. He thought he heard Gordon Sloane's voice in the background.

Marvia agreed to meet him at the Fat Lady in downtown Oakland. She had some things to tell him, but they could wait for an hour. There was nothing he could do in a Boeing six miles over Colorado.

6

It was raining in Oakland and the air was cold and damp, but Lindsey's blue Volvo 544 had started without hesitation. He parked on Washington Street and pushed open the cut-glass front door of the Fat Lady. Marvia was sitting at the bar. She swung around as Lindsey came through the door. In an instant she was off her bar-stool and in his arms. She felt warm against him. He was home.

On a chilly night Lindsey savored the double warmth of an Irish coffee. Marvia was nursing something in a tall glass. They sat at a table in a half-concealed booth. The bar was jammed with dress-for-success types unwinding after their day's work.

Marvia did not look happy. She held both Lindsey's hands in hers. He said, 'Marvia, something's the matter.'

She didn't pull any punches. 'Ben Zinowicz is out of prison.'

'That's no surprise. I've already crossed trails with him.' He told her about Cletus Berry and his conversation with Lovisi. 'But I thought he was in San Quentin for the long haul. How could they let somebody like *that* out?'

'They're cleaning house again, dumping prisoners to make room for more prisoners. Three strikes and all that.'

Lindsey pulled one hand free from Marvia's and squeezed tighter with the other. 'He killed that poor kid in Berkeley. He killed my bloody father! He crippled that poor woman, that radio announcer, Sojourner Strength. He put her in a wheelchair. He shot me, and he was going after Mother when you guys finally caught him.'

She touched his cheek with her free hand. 'You knew about his plea-bargain.'

Lindsey half-moaned, 'Sure.'

'The navy wouldn't prosecute him for what happened in Korea. It was just too many years — the evidence was flimsy; the whole thing was conjecture.'

'How can you say that?' Lindsey demanded.

'*You* know he did it and *I* know he did it, but the navy just didn't want to get involved in a case halfway around the world that was almost forty years old. To keep their records clean, they just didn't want to get involved.'

'Anchors aweigh.' The words tasted bitter in his mouth.

'And you know he had an alibi for killing that boy behind the comic book store. His weird friend with the weird name — '

'Francis Francis. I had a nasty encounter with that one, too.'

'Well, *he's* dead. And Nathan ben Zinowicz wasn't above pinning everything he could on Francis.'

'So the long and the short of it is, he's free as a bird. And back here, too, I suppose.'

'They had to parole him back here. That's the law. But he's not quite as free as a bird. He didn't insist on serving his time to the last tick of the clock and then walk away. Ben Zinowicz is on parole, and I know his parole officer. So that's something, anyway.'

'Yes, I suppose.' The warmth of the room and the pleasure of being with her surrounded by dark wood and old paintings had evaporated. 'Can I find out this parole officer's name?'

'I'll give you his name. You can go talk to him. He's a good man, an ex-cop. You'll get along.'

'*But?*'

'Let's get out of here. Let's go home and go to bed.'

'No.' Lindsey shook his head. 'You haven't told me everything. I know I'm not the world's most perceptive guy, Marvia, but I know you haven't told me everything.'

Marvia bit her lip. 'He has a job. He's the executive secretary of the World Fund for Indigent Artists.'

★　★　★

They stopped for take-out on the way to Marvia's flat in Berkeley. The turret in the Victorian on Oxford Street had become Lindsey's favorite refuge. When he was there with Marvia, Lindsey felt safe, insulated from the violence and madness of the world.

Lindsey didn't have much appetite tonight. He had to talk with Roger St. John Cooke or with Cynthia Cooke, maybe with both of them. They had a material interest in Albert Crocker Vansittart's death benefits, and Lindsey fully expected them to play hardball in their efforts to collect four million dollars. And the knowledge that Nathan ben Zinowicz was now associated with the Cookes was like a hot dagger in the side of Lindsey's skull.

Marvia put the take-out food in the refrigerator in the common kitchen. Lindsey said he wanted to take a walk. They walked up to the Berkeley rose garden, and looked at the view. They could see across Berkeley to the Bay and to San Francisco across the water, the lights of the bridges and of the city's buildings glittering like Hollywood special effects.

Marvia told Lindsey about the Tahoe and Berkeley end of the Vansittart investigation. Finally the UNR people had gotten a usable fiber-optic probe to the wrecked helicopter. The feds were involved, and that helped ease the costs of the project. The chopper was lying upside-down on the silty bottom of the lake. Getting the probe to the helicopter had been only the first hurdle. Getting a clear view through the Plexiglas bubble came next, and even once that was achieved the results were ambiguous.

Fabia Rabinowitz had tapes from the probe and she was working to clear them up. She also had Jamie Wilkerson's Handycam tape and had started sharpening the definition of that as well. Marvia had seen the tapes, and described them to Lindsey. The crabs had got to Albert Crocker Vansittart, and the flesh was coming off him in strips. It was a horrifying sight, but in a way it was helpful, because the probe caught a picture of his skull. It was badly bashed in.

'But that doesn't prove anything,' Marvia said. 'That might have happened in the crash. John O'Farrell, the pilot, came out of the crash with a broken leg.

The same impact that snapped his leg bones could just as well have broken Vansittart's skull.'

'Or maybe not.' Lindsey was getting interested. Sherlock Holmes had found that puzzles were more interesting than cocaine. Hobart Lindsey found them more appealing than depression. 'What if O'Farrell killed Vansittart? I'm just posing the question.'

'Okay, Bart — how would he do that? And why?'

'Vansittart was an old man. He would have been strapped into the chopper. O'Farrell was half his age; a strong, agile guy. You saw how he came up that cable, freezing water, broken leg and all. In the helicopter he was on his own turf; he knew exactly what he was doing. He could have whacked Vansittart on the bean with a wrench or a crowbar. That would account for the broken skull just as well as an injury when the chopper crashed. Better, I think.'

'Possible,' Marvia admitted.

'Or,' Lindsey went on, 'he could have shot him in the head. That would account for the broken skull, too. Or maybe he shot him in the heart or in the belly. The bullet killed him, and the crash and the broken skull were gratuitous.'

'Hah. Some gratuity. Why did the helicopter crash?'

Lindsey pondered, then said, 'Two possibilities. If O'Farrell shot Vansittart, the bullet might have gone right through him and wrecked the controls, cut a cable or whatever. We saw on Jamie's tape how the copter shuddered before it started to fall.'

Marvia conceded as much.

'Okay. Possibility number two, the crash was *staged* to look like an accident. If O'Farrell murdered Vansittart some-where up there a few thousand feet over the Sierras, what the heck was he going to do with the body? Throw it out of the chopper? That might be embarrassing. Even if nobody found Vansittart in those mountains for a long time, there would have been questions, hey? Things like appointment books, hotel reservations, flight manifests. You don't just take off with two people in a helicopter and land with only one and nobody's going to think that's odd.' Lindsey was gesturing with both hands. 'If O'Farrell hadn't dumped Vansittart's body — if he touched down smoothly in Reno — how in the world could he explain this fresh corpse? Answer: crash the chopper into the lake. O'Farrell gets out safely, Vansittart's body is disposed of, everything on the up-and-up. Just a tragic accident.'

He took Marvia's hand and resumed walking. 'I don't think O'Farrell figured on coming out of it with a broken leg; but once it happened, all the better. O'Farrell comes out looking like a hero.'

They had reached Marvia's house again. Her Mustang and Lindsey's restored Volvo 544 were parked nose-and-tail at the curb. Marvia said, 'One problem, Bart. There's no evidence that O'Farrell killed Vansittart. Why would he have any reason to kill him?'

Lindsey grinned wryly. 'Just a theory.'

They climbed the stairs to Marvia's flat. She put on a CD of Ellington indigos and they got undressed and climbed under the Raggedy Ann comforter on Marvia's bed.

They shared early-morning coffee at a bistro on Shattuck Avenue. Lindsey said, 'I want to talk to Nathan ben Zinowicz's parole officer.'

Marvia took a calling card from her wallet and turned it over and wrote the information on the back. The parole officer was called Dave Jones and his office was in downtown Oakland.

* * *

David Jones was dark and muscular but soft-spoken. He'd cultivated the soft tone to make his charges listen carefully to what he had to tell them. 'We can't follow them around like watchdogs,' Jones said. 'Too many of them and too few of us. We have to rely on voluntary compliance mostly, and spot checks, and make them report in regularly. But it's all pretty much a crap-shoot, I won't try and kid you.'

Lindsey grunted. 'What about Nathan ben Zinowicz?'

'Recent parolee. We just had a meeting last week.'

Involuntarily, Lindsey clenched his fists, his fingernails cutting into his palms. 'I thought the victims had rights. Don't they hold hearings, give people a chance to have their say?'

'That's the procedure. What was your connection with this case?'

Lindsey told him, struggling to hold himself in check when he described his father's death on the deck of *USS Lewiston* in the Sea of Japan, and his own encounters with Nathan ben Zinowicz so many years later.

When Lindsey finished speaking, Jones walked to a file cabinet and extracted a manila folder. He laid it on the desk between them. 'I can't show you this material; Mr. ben Zinowicz has privacy rights even though he is still technically under control of the Department of Corrections. I probably shouldn't be talking with you at all, but Marvia Plum is a very old, very dear friend. She's mentioned you many times. You going to marry her?'

Lindsey hesitated, then said yes.

'She's a wonderful person, and her son, Jamie — '

'I know that. I want to talk about ben Zinowicz.'

Jones opened the folder and scanned its contents, turning the pages slowly. Finally he said, 'What do you want to tell me?'

'That he belongs behind bars.'

'I certainly understand your feelings, but with his plea bargain I'm kind of surprised that he did any time at all. Second, he was an exemplary prisoner in Q. Worked in the personnel office, taught literacy classes, kept his nose clean. Not one beef in forty-two months. I'm surprised he didn't get out sooner.'

Lindsey suppressed a groan.

'Third, he has a first-rate job now. He reports for work every day, and his employer gives him an A-plus rating. He comes in here for his little progress meetings. With his tweedy outfits and thick glasses and that little gray beard of his, he looks like a college professor.'

'He ought to. He *was* one until he . . . ' Lindsey paused.

Jones pointed a blunt-tipped finger. 'I

wish my caseload was full of Nathan ben Zinowiczes. Is there anything else you want?' He looked at his wristwatch. 'I've got a meeting.'

Lindsey gave it one more try. 'Don't you think it's odd? I mean, we know this man's history, both in Korea and here.'

'I don't know anything about Korea. Personally I know what you told me, but officially I only know what's in the folder. And the only thing the folder says about Korea is lieutenant commander, US navy, navy cross, purple heart, honorable discharge. The rest, I don't know.'

Lindsey wanted to scream. This was why people bought Uzis and went berserk. 'This killer is out of prison; he goes to work for the WFIA. Suddenly Albert Crocker Vansittart dies under suspicious circumstances, and WFIA is mentioned in his insurance policy for four million bucks. Don't you smell something rotten about that?'

'No, sir, I don't. I think maybe you're being paranoid. I have to warn you, Mr. Lindsey, not to harass Dr. ben Zinowicz. He has rights. Leave him alone.'

7

Lindsey wanted to spend another night with Marvia, but he'd promised Mother. He phoned Marvia, promising to call her again tomorrow. Then he set about planning his next moves.

Returning to the International Surety office in Walnut Creek had not raised his spirits. Mathilde Wilbur, his old friend and mentor, was retired. International Surety's outer office was presided over by the blonde and spiteful Kari Fielding; the inner office, by the loathsome Elmer Mueller.

Lindsey made his way to the desk that was reserved for him. He filed a brief report on his meeting with Jones through KlameNet/Plus. Then prepared to do what he had to do. He needed to talk with either of the Cookes at the World Fund for Indigent Artists, and he needed to talk with J.B. Harkins, late of the Chicago *Inter-Ocean, Daily News,* and *Sun-Times*, and author of *Baseball Stars of 1952.*

He rang the World Fund first. Thankfully the voice that answered was not the arrogant supercilious tone of Nathan ben Zinowicz. He identified himself and asked to speak with Mr. Cooke.

Cooke took the call and suggested that they meet the following day. 'No need to come up to the office for a first informal chat. What about one o'clock? And I'll see if my darling is available. Shall we say Liberté — on Sutter Street? Oh, of course, in San Francisco. See you then. Just ask for my table; Marthe holds one for me every day.'

Lindsey rang off and made a note in his pocket organizer. Then he looked up another number. The woman who answered his call managed to get more good cheer into the words *Shady Oaks* than a department store Santa could get into *Merry Christmas*. Lindsey asked if he could speak with J.B. Harkind. ' . . . and would you tell Mr. Harkins that this is a friend of Maude Markham's, from Chicago?'

'Oh, you're calling all the way from Chicago? Mr. Harkins will be so pleased. Please hold. I'll try to be as quick as I can, but you know Mr. Harkins is quite elderly, and our seniors don't always move as quickly as they once did.'

Lindsey waited patiently.

Harkins sounded old, his voice a dry rasp. But he sounded as if he still had all his marbles. He said, 'Nurse Ratchet there says I have a call from Chicago. You a friend of Maude Markham's?'

'Yes, I — '

'Well, any friend of Maude Markham's can go take a good flying splat as far as I'm concerned!'

Lindsey heard the receiver crash into its cradle at the Shady Oaks Retirement Villas in Livermore. He groaned. Across the room, Kari Fielding shot him a hostile glance.

He hit redial and got the cheery voice again. He asked if she would get Mr. Harkins on the phone once more, but first explain to him that he wasn't really a *friend* of Maude Markham's; he'd just got Harkins' location from Maude Markham, who was a crusty unpleasant individual, and he was eager to talk with the author of *Baseball Stars of 1952*.

Nurse Ratchet said, 'If I fetch Mr. Harkins a second time, you must promise me faithfully not to get him upset again.'

Lindsey promised to be very soothing. He could hear the two voices engaged in dialog. Finally he heard Harkins grunt, then speak into the telephone.

'I better apologize. Lost my temper for a sec. Maude was a good old broad. Glad to hear she's still in circulation. She still working for the *Sun-Times*, is she?'

'Uh, yes.'

'Not really a bad soul. I went off to World War II, you know. She knew how to give a soldier boy a happy fare-thee-well. Say, I don't suppose she looks too much like that nowadays, does she? I know I sure don't.'

'Mr. Harkins, I was wondering if I might come out there to Livermore see you about your book?'

'Are you nuts?'

'No, I'm not actually in Chicago. I'm in

Walnut Creek, about forty minutes from you.'

There was a silence as Harkins assimilated that piece of information. Then, 'How 'bout tomorrow?'

'Uh — I have a luncheon meeting in San Francisco tomorrow. How about the next day?'

'Goddamn, sonny! If you're going to be in San Francisco for lunch you can come out here afterwards. Tell you what, you come on out here and take me out to dinner someplace. I like good Mexican; they never serve it here. You come out here seven o'clock. I'll be in the lobby. Bring that book. You got a copy?'

'Uh — yes, I — '

'Seven o'clock. Goodbye.'

*   *   *

It was dark out by the time Lindsey got home. Gordon Sloane's silver-gray Oldsmobile stood in the driveway, and all the lights were on in the house. He found Sloane and Mother waiting for him in the living room.

129

Mother gave Lindsey a kiss. She asked, 'How was your day?'

'Mixed. Yours? Gordon?' He shook Sloane's hand. Gordon Sloane said, 'We have something to tell you, Bart. Your mother and I have decided to get married.'

Mother put her hand on Lindsey's sleeve. She was wearing nail polish. Another first for her, at least as far as he could remember. She said, 'I hoped you'd be pleased, Bart. Will you give us your blessing? I know you must have feelings for your father, but . . . '

'I never knew my father.'

'I was so young when we were married. Just a little girl. And we were only married a few months when he died. Don't you think I'm entitled to — '

Lindsey put his arms around her. 'You are, Mother. You're entitled to some companionship. Love.'

Sloane stood behind Mother. He held out his hand and Lindsey shook it, then said, 'Your mother tells me that you and Marvia are planning to marry. What would you think of a double wedding?'

'Uh — I'm not sure when we're going to do it. Have you set a date? Have you — '

'I thought we could talk about everything,' Mother said, gesturing vaguely.

'Marvia would have to be here.'

Sloane nodded. 'Of course. I think the four of us should get together and make our plans. If that's all right.'

Mother said, 'Bart, let's go out and celebrate. Just the three of us. Gordon has made reservations.'

'I hope you don't mind,' Sloane added.

Lindsey excused himself. He showered and put on a good suit, then came back into the living room quietly. Mother and Gordon were seated side by side on the couch. Sloane stood up when Lindsey came in. He said, 'We've been saving this.' He unwrapped a champagne bottle and opened it skillfully. There were already glasses for three on the table. He poured champagne for them and they drank.

Sloane looked at his watch. 'I think we should be off.'

* * *

Dinner was northern Italian. They had wine with their meal. They talked about what they were going to do after Sloane and Mother were married. Sloane owned a condo in Walnut Creek. He and his wife had lived there before her death. Once Mother moved in, Sloane hoped that she would bring back the woman's touch.

Mother glowed like a bride. 'We've already talked about selling the house,' she said. 'Unless you want to stay in it, Bart. Would you and Marvia want to stay in the house? Would Jamie come to live with you?'

Lindsey shook his head. 'I don't know. Marvia and I still have to decide what we're going to do. Her ex-husband turned up a while ago. He's remarried, there's no problem there, but he tried to interfere with Jamie. Marvia and I will probably have to talk to a lawyer before we're married, to make sure that Mr. Wilkerson doesn't come back into the picture.'

'Will Marvia keep her job?' Sloane asked. 'Can she move out here and still be

132

a Berkeley police officer?'

'We haven't talked about that. We haven't worked things out.' Lindsey was uncomfortable with Sloane's questions, because he didn't have answers for himself. He asked, 'Have you set a date, Mother, Gordon?'

'We haven't,' Sloane said, 'but we want to. That's why we both thought that you and Marvia might — '

Lindsey nodded. 'I'll talk to Marvia about it.' Then, 'Mother, do you think you'll keep working?'

'I think so. Now that I'm back in the real world, I couldn't just stay home again all day. When I think of all the lost years, wandering off into old magazines, TV shows, dreams and memories . . . I did miss your father so, Hobart.'

'I know, Mother.'

'Well, I have a few years left. I don't want that to happen again. You can't imagine what it's like, after all these years, to be *part* of something; to do something useful.'

★　★　★

When they got home, Lindsey phoned Marvia and told her about the evening and asked when they could sit down and make serious plans.

The next day he drove into the city and parked in the garage underneath Union Square. He got to Liberté early and spent half an hour window-shopping. He checked his Seiko, then entered Liberté. The restaurant was down a flight of stairs and decorated to look like the inside of a cave. Lindsey asked for Mr. Cooke's table and an Asian woman in a floor-length, drop-dead dress nodded knowingly and led him through a maze of pillars.

Roger St. John Cooke stood up as Lindsey approached. He extended a manicured hand. He wore a light brown mustache and a small beard. His suit was double-breasted, black with white pinstripes, and had clearly been made for him. They shook hands.

Cooke said, 'Hobart Lindsey, Mrs. Cooke. Cynthia.'

Cynthia extended her hand. Lindsey resisted an impulse to bend over the hand and mutter something in a Bela Lugosi accent. Instead, he just shook her hand. He thought she looked like Hillary Clinton trying to look like Princess Di — or maybe the other way around.

Lindsey felt pressure on the back of his knees and let himself be seated.

The waiter said, 'Will the gentleman enjoy a beverage?'

Lindsey shot a quick look at the Cookes. A small blue bottle of imported mineral water stood before each of them, beside a crystal glass with ice cubes and lemon. Lindsey said, 'I'll have the same, please.' The waiter departed.

Roger St. John Cooke said, 'This is about the Vansittart policy, of course. I thought this would be a nicer place to get together than the office.'

Lindsey thought so too, if only because it saved him from having to lay eyes on Nathan ben Zinowicz.

As Lindsey's mineral water arrived, Cynthia Cooke said silkily, 'Of course, we were heartbroken when we learned of Albert's death. He was a dear friend.'

'I didn't know that.'

'More of a family friend,' Roger said.

'Bertie Junior and I were roommates at Stanford. Class of . . . ' He gave a small, self-deprecating laugh. 'Let's just say, a long time ago.'

Lindsey was surprised. 'I didn't know he had any immediate survivors. If so, I wonder if — '

He didn't get any further. 'Poor Bert. He was killed in a tragic accident. Broken neck. A football injury a long time ago. Stanford versus Cal, of course. I was on the squad, too. But I was just a scrub; Bert was going on to great things. He would have stayed in the family business, I'm sure of it. I don't think his dad ever got over his death.'

The waiter was back. He handed only Lindsey a menu. Cynthia smiled. 'Victor knows our preference. I would recommend the special. The special is always good at Liberté.'

'Sure. Fine.' Victor withdrew. 'What about Bert's mother?'

Roger shook his head sadly. 'After Bert died . . . well, I don't think it had been the happiest of marriages. Not like ours, dear, eh?' He took his wife's hand and pressed it to his lips. Lindsey didn't comment. 'No, Albert Senior and Anna were not the ideal couple. She drank, I'm afraid, and he . . . well, he loved women perhaps a bit too much, if you understand me.'

Cynthia picked up her glass and sipped mineral water. She gazed adoringly at her husband, waiting for him to resume.

'I think that Anna just stayed with Albert Senior for Bertie's sake,' Roger said. 'Once Bertie was gone . . . well, the marriage didn't last long. And once that was over, well, Anna went for a spin one day in her hot little Ferrari that she kept in St. Tropez, and she may have had a drink or so too many, and she got dizzy, and . . . well, it was all a tragedy. Smashed into a giant palm tree. Wrecked the car, of course, and threw poor Anna right out. She bounced off the tree trunk, too — right through the windshield, across the hood, against the tree trunk. Dead, of course.'

Lindsey bit his lip to keep himself from saying anything. Too many people were getting dizzy from the sunlight and experiencing fatal accidents.

Cynthia put her glass back down. 'You're never going to find this mythical houri of Vansittart's, you know. The old goat bedded everything in skirts. That was in the days when women wore skirts and you could tell them from men.'

Lindsey blinked.

'There's no way you can track her down,' she repeated. 'Probably never was such a person to start with. Didn't those cheap-jack artists keep swipe files? They copied each other's pictures, they painted over movie stills, they combined models, everything.'

'You know a lot about this.'

'I do. You'd be surprised at some of the things I know.'

Roger said, 'My wife holds a master's degree in commercial art.' He glanced proudly at his sweetie.

'You'll never find that woman,' Cynthia said. 'The fund is entitled to that insurance policy, and the sooner your company pays up, the better.'

8

J.B. Harkins was waiting when Lindsey arrived at Shady Oaks, good as his word. Harkins was tall, bespectacled, and cadaverously thin. His hair and mustache were white, and his threadbare clothing could have been a parody of Roger Cooke's.

The old man said, 'Let's get the heck out of this joint and find some decent grub. I hate the pap here.'

Lindsey didn't know anything about Livermore, but they managed to find a Mexican place that looked pretty good. They left the Volvo in the street.

Inside the restaurant, Lindsey and Harkins got a table and Harkins said, 'You want something from me, you better make me happy. A whiskey sour will make me happy.'

Lindsey looked around, spotted a waitress and signaled. He asked Harkins, 'Will you tell me about your book?'

'What's to tell? I had the hots for Maude Markham. So I figured, maybe we should get married. I was covering the Cubs in those days for the *Chicago Daily News*. Pretty good old paper. Summer of '51.' He downed the second half of his whiskey sour. 'Get me another one of those, would you? It's a lousy drink but it beats hell out anything they serve out there at the graveyard.'

Lindsey signaled the waitress. To Harkins he said, 'I think we should get some food.'

The waitress brought Harkins' second drink along with their food. Harkins dug into his dinner. The taco came with rice and beans, a green salad, and a covered dish of corn tortillas. He demolished half of it in a rush, then sat back and sighed, rubbing his belly. 'Can't tell you what a difference this makes, mac. But I do appreciate it.'

'What about your book, Mr. Harkins?' Lindsey placed his copy of *Baseball Stars of 1952* carefully on a folded napkin.

'Yep, this is it all right. Took me a week to write this bugger. Would have done one every year if poor old Kleinhoffer'd managed to keep his company going.'

'You knew his real name?'

'Everybody knew that those names they took were just to sound like real Murricans. Nobody took that stuff seriously.' He turned the book around and around, studying it.

'Do you know who the artist was?' Lindsey asked. 'I can't find any art credit on the book. On any of them, in fact. Walter Paige's — Werner Kleinhoffer's — granddaughter gave them to me. They all look like one artist's work. But there's no signature, no art credit on the books.'

'No signature?' He pointed at one of the sketches on the cover of *Baseball Stars of 1952*, one of the miniature baseball parks that surrounded the faces of the baseball stars. Hidden in the line work and almost too small to see was a drawing of a gun with two bullets coming from its muzzle.

Lindsey jumped in his seat. 'I see it, yes. But why a gun? And why those bullets?'

'No, no, young fellow. Those aren't

bullets. They're BBs. That's the artist's signature. BB. He called himself Bob Brown. His real name was Benjamin Bruninski. BB. Don't you get it?'

'I get it. Lindsey took the book back from Harkins. 'He did all the covers for Paige?'

'Far as I know. I didn't have that much to do with that Paige outfit. Werner called the *Daily News* office and asked for me. Said he read my stuff every day in the paper, really liked my writing, how would I like to do a book for his company? I had the hots for Maude Markham, you know, and wanted to pick up some extra moolah. If that book company hadn't gone belly-up, I'd have probably made enough in a year or two to marry her. Would have made a better wife than any I ever had.'

'Did you know a model who posed for Bob Brown? She was on several of his book covers for Paige. She was on *Death in the Ditch*. Blonde woman, green eyes, very busty, very beautiful. At least, she was blonde on that book; she was a brunette or redhead on the others.'

'Sounds like hot stuff. I wouldn't know. Only talked with Benny Boy a couple of times, about the cover for *Baseball Stars*. I had to tell him who the players were that I was writing about. The clubs sent us publicity stills and Benny used those to paint from.' He closed his eyes, then reeled off a roll-call of player's names. Then he took the book back and pointed to one of the stadium sketches. 'Old Benny Boy, you know, he was a baseball man himself. Really knew his stuff. You see these ballparks? Oh, the best ones are gone now. They build these ridiculous domes and things now. No character to 'em.'

He picked up his fork and speared a slice of tomato in a pink creamy sauce. He ate it, then he said, 'You see this ballpark here? See, all these parks are big league parks except this one. This here is a minor league park — Pelican Stadium, New Orleans, Louisiana. Your eyes are glazing over, boy. You are not a baseball man, I can see that. New Orleans Pelicans played there, and the New Orleans Stars, Negro League team. Crazy ballpark.

Gone now. All they build nowadays are giant spare tires with ballfields in the middle.'

Lindsey put the book away carefully and paid for their food. On the way back to Harkins' retirement home, he asked if Harkins had any idea where Bob Brown, Benjamin Bruninski, might be today. If he was still alive.

Harkins looked at Lindsey. 'You're quite the detective, aren't you, sonny?'

'I'm trying to find him.'

'Now why would that artist make that nice cover for my book, and all of the players are big league players and all of the ballparks are big league ballparks except for one? How stupid are you, mac?'

At the Shady Oaks Retirement Villas, Lindsey walked into the lobby with Harkins. Harkins said, 'You come back and take me out for another good meal, will you?'

9

Fabia Rabinowitz had moved back to the UC computer center after finishing her assignment on loan to the Pacific Film Archive. Her workplace was a combination office and computer lab. A custom-built processor stood on her desk, a printer beside it. A VCR was cabled into the processor. The walls were lined with shelves of manuals and computer magazines and stacks of printouts. The window looked out on Sproul Plaza, where students moved briskly between classes in the heavy rain.

Fabia Rabinowitz, dark-haired and elegant, sat at the computer keyboard. The others were crowded into the small room: Hobart Lindsey, and Marvia Plum and Willie Fergus in uniform. Fergus's was the only new face to Lindsey. He was about Lindsey's height and clearly older, with gray in his crinkled black hair, but in good shape.

Fabia gestured casually at her computer. 'What we've got here is some fancy software that we tried out a while ago on those old movies Mr. MacReedy from the retirement center provided. We were trying to deconstruct the footage to determine if a certain famous actor had been replaced in mid-career by a double.'

'And he had,' Lindsey volunteered.

From a drawer she extracted two videocassettes. 'These are high-quality copies of the tape of the UNR fiber-optic probe of the helicopter wreck, and Jamie's tape of the helicopter crash.' She slid a cassette into the VCR and punched a few buttons on the device and a few more on the computer keyboard. The monitor screen came to life. 'I'm going to take these in reverse sequence, because the fiber-optic tape shows us what to look for in Jamie's tape.'

The monitor screen showed an eerie dark green scene. 'This is the bottom of Lake Tahoe, too deep for natural light to penetrate. We see this by a tracer light on the cable.' Suddenly the scene brightened. 'At this point the operators turned on the main light. We can see the crashed and sunken helicopter. It's lying on its main rotor. The tail is broken off and lies beside the major wreckage. We can see that the Plexiglas bubble has been crushed by the weight of the wreck. Now, the probe is going to move.'

The scene shifted dizzyingly, then stabilized. 'Here we see the downrigger cable that was attached by the *Tahoe Tailflipper*. The captain of the *Tailflipper* was trying to save the occupants of the helicopter, of course; but in fact it was this, we believe, that caused the helicopter to invert as it sank.'

'That cable's all that saved John O'Farrell,' Fergus put in.

The monitor screen showed the inside of the helicopter bubble. The probe had crept in like a water snake, powered by fractional horsepower motors and guided from the surface of Lake Tahoe. The light glinted off a metal surface, then moved on toward a grisly figure.

Fergus said, 'Hold it there. Can you back that up?'

Fabia clicked at her keyboard. Frame by frame, the probe backed away from Albert Crocker Vansittart's remains.

'Stop!' Fergus barked. The glinting metal object looked like a bit of dull mirror surrounded by green murk. 'Can you sharpen that up?'

Fabia's hands flew over the computer keyboard like Liberace's over ivories. Miraculously, the image on the screen grew clear. Fergus had been jotting notes. He used his pen as a pointer, tapping it against the glass face of the monitor. 'That's a tire-iron.'

Lindsey started. 'Why would they need one of those in a helicopter? It doesn't even have tires, does it?'

'Not those old Bells. That's an old Model 47, upgraded and modified to civilian use, and it still has landing skids, not wheels.'

'Well, then — ?'

'Dr. Rabinowitz, can you step that forward again? Just a few seconds' worth.'

The monitor image moved again. Eventually the body of Albert Crocker Vansittart became visible, hanging upside down by its safety belt. There was some flesh left on his face. Lindsey's stomach lurched. He could have dealt with either a complete face or a bare skull, but he was not prepared for the horror that appeared. 'My God!' he gasped.

Willie said, 'Mr. Lindsey, you think you're up to this? You don't have to watch.'

Lindsey gulped. 'Sure. I'm okay now.'

Fabia rolled a mouse around a rubber pad, blowing up segments of the screen. 'This is what I think you wanted to see.'

What was left of Albert Crocker Vansittart's face filled the screen. Fabia Rabinowitz hit some keys. The face rotated 180 degrees. It seemed to stare at them.

Willie said, 'That's what I wanted. See that hole in Vansittart's skull? That's not an impact fracture from the chopper crash. It's a puncture wound. He was struck, and it was the tire-iron that was used to strike him. Maybe once with the flat of the shaft to stun him, then a poking-type blow that penetrated his skull. That's what killed him. And the tire iron, I'll bet my stripes, was the murder weapon.'

'Then the killer was O'Farrell,' Lindsey said.

'It had to be. I think I'd better get on the horn to my boss and have him call the Placer Sheriff's office. Can I use your phone, Dr. Rabinowitz?'

She handed him a telephone. He placed the call and spoke briefly. There was a silence that dragged on, then he spoke a few more words and lowered the receiver. He looked around, then said, 'What about Jamie's tape?'

Fabia popped the cassette out of the VCR and inserted another in its place. Lindsey watched the familiar footage of Hakeem White and the wriggling salmon. Then the image panned diagonally to capture the image of the oncoming helicopter. The Handycam's built-in microphone caught the sound of the helicopter's rotors. The camera followed its descent. The copter splashed into the lake and almost at once began to founder.

Jamie had caught most of the action on

his Handycam. The sequence ended with O'Farrell's words, 'I've got to get him out of there! It's Mr. Vansittart!'

The monitor screen went blank. When the whir of the rewinding tape stopped, Fabia said, 'Now I'm going to run the tape again, stopping at crucial moments to show you a couple of blowups and refined images.'

The tape started again. As the helicopter dropped toward the lake, Fabia froze the image. Lindsey could see the helicopter and its Plexiglas bubble. The rotor blades were a frozen blur. Fabia played her keyboard-and-mouse game. A frame appeared around the bubble. Then the image within the frame sprang toward Lindsey until it filled the monitor screen. Lindsey could see two shadowy figures inside the bubble.

Fabia advanced the tape, frame by frame. The image on the monitor became more clearly defined. 'Watch this.'

Lindsey could clearly distinguish two figures inside the bubble. The one closer to the camera held a long, thin object in his hand. The tape advanced, frame by frame, with nightmare slowness. The hand came up. The second figure, further from the camera, raised both its hands. The object fell across the second man's temple. As the second man slumped, the first man drew back his arm, shifted his grip on the long object and jabbed it, point first, into the second man's skull. Then he dropped the object and moved his hands back to the controls of the helicopter.

By now the copter was close to the surface of the lake, some forty or fifty feet in the air. The Handycam followed it down to the surface. As the copter splashed into the lake, Fabia slowed the tape again. Lindsey saw the two men in the Plexiglas bubble. One was slumped in his seat, unmoving. The other was struggling frantically with the copter's controls. As the machine neared the water he gave up on the controls and struggled frantically to undo his safety belt.

Then the copter splashed, foundered, slowly sank. There was confusion on the *Tahoe Tailflipper,* much of it caught by ace cameraman Jamie Wilkerson. The tape ended and again rewound.

Willie Fergus said, 'Well I'll be damned. I haven't seen anything like that since Jack Ruby shot Lee Harvey Oswald. I'd better phone Reno again. This is going to be a mess. We'll have to ask the California police to hold O'Farrell while we get a warrant in Nevada. That son of a bitch — he'll probably fight extradition.'

Marvia stood up. 'Don't be too sure of that, Willie. I'm not so sure the crime took place in Nevada. The copter apparently sank in Nevada water, but it was coming from the west, from California. Jamie's tape shows the crime being committed as the copter approaches the *Tahoe Tailflipper*. The crime might have been committed in California.

'Let me get on that phone. I'm going to alert Placer County. Let's pick him up in California, since that's where he is now. See if he can travel. If not, put a guard on him right in the hospital. Then we'll see who gets jurisdiction. And I'm sure that the Placer County Sheriff has been talking to the Coast Guard and the FBI and half a million other feds.'

She took the phone and placed her call. She'd barely put the telephone down when it rang with an incoming call for Sergeant Willie Fergus.

He took the handset, listened, grunted, then returned the handset to its cradle. He looked around at the others. His face had gone from a rich chocolate brown to a sickly gray. 'O'Farrell checked out of the hospital this morning.'

O'Farrell had been in a private room. His broken leg had been set, and he'd recovered from the shock and exposure. X-ray and MRI examinations had shown a concussion, but that was clearing up. With the broken leg in a cast and a few visible bruises, the man had been ready to travel.

A friend had arrived with a station wagon. O'Farrell had signed himself out. The friend had not been identified, and apparently nobody on the hospital staff had particularly noticed him or bothered to note the license number of the station wagon. An orderly had helped O'Farrell and his friend to the wagon, rolling O'Farrell along in a wheelchair, helping him to make the difficult move from the wheelchair into the backspace of the wagon, where he could sit with his broken leg outstretched. The station wagon had a California license, the orderly remembered that. But not the brand of the wagon.

Willie addressed the others. 'Okay, there's already an APB out for O'Farrell. Washoe has it in effect for all of Nevada, in case they headed down toward Reno and Carson City. The sooner we get out the word, the smaller the area they're likely to be in. Marvia, Placer County is putting one on the line for California, in case they headed back toward Sacramento — or anyplace else, of course. O'Farrell is going to be pretty conspicuous with his leg in a cast. And he won't be very mobile, either. That's our best bet. No way he can just mix and mingle with the public. He'll have to hole up.' He turned to Lindsey. 'I guess that settles things for you, sir. Even without a body, the probe proved that Vansittart is dead, and — '

Lindsey held up his hand. 'How do we

know that was Vansittart? We saw a body in the helicopter. We know it wasn't O'Farrell because he survived. And he told Captain MacKenzie on the fishing boat that his passenger was Vansittart. Suppose it was somebody else? Do you just take O'Farrell's word? Especially now that we know he's a killer?'

Fergus nodded. 'You're right. I should have thought of that.' He looked up, locking eyes with Lindsey. 'But in any case, I think you're out of this for now. The coroner will have to make a ruling on Vansittart, and since the body is in Nevada, it will be the Washoe County coroner, not Placer County.'

'Can you tape that whole thing?' he asked Fabia. 'Everything you showed us, ma'am? And — when the time comes, you'll be willing to appear in court?'

'Certainly.' She nodded. 'I can do all that. And appear in court if I have to.'

'What about you, Mr. Lindsey? You and Sergeant Plum were both witnesses to the helicopter crash. You're as close to witnesses to the crime itself as there are.'

Lindsey shot a look at Marvia. 'I just

saw the copter crash. Then I saw O'Farrell climb back up that cable.'

'That's right,' Marvia agreed. 'I don't think we can add anything useful. But both boys saw the crash, and Captain MacKenzie.'

'Well just in case, I think I'd better call in again,' Fergus said. 'Then I expect they'll want me back in Tahoe. I don't see what more there is to do down here. Dr. Rabinowitz — again, this is fantastic work. We'll want to get it into evidence a.s.a.p. How soon do you think you can have a package ready for us?'

'I think I can still sharpen the images up a little bit. Give me a week and I'll have a package for you.'

Fergus nodded and shook her hand. 'Marvia — you want to have a cup of coffee with me? I need to talk with you a little more, then I think I'm out of here.'

Marvia nodded. To Lindsey she said, 'This is just cop stuff. Give me a call later, all right?' The group scattered.

Lindsey reached Marvia later by telephone and they planned dinner. He drove back to the I.S. office in Walnut Creek and caught up on paperwork. Then he went home and changed into fresh clothes and drove back to Berkeley.

10

Lindsey didn't have much of an appetite, so Marvia suggested a sushi and robata bar on Solano Avenue.

He told Marvia about his dinner with Mother and Gordon Sloane.

'What kind of double wedding? Bart, if we do this, I want it to be just us. I'm sorry. Your mother can be there, of course, if you want her to. But I don't want a fuss. I want to keep it small and quiet.'

Lindsey blinked. 'All right.' The conversation was getting away from him. The topics were swirling like snowflakes in a blizzard. Their wedding, Mother's wedding, the helicopter crash, Vansittart, the Cookes, John O'Farrell.

'Bertie Vansittart,' he blurted suddenly. 'Albert Vansittart, Junior. Wasn't Vansittart a confirmed bachelor? Wasn't that what CNN said?'

'Sure they did.'

'Roger Cooke told me that he was college roommates with Vansittart's son. He fed me this line about his wonderful roommate the football hero. Then Albert Junior was killed. Broke his neck on the gridiron.'

Marvia watched him with a look of intense concentration.

'Then his mother, Albert Vansittart, Senior's wife — she was always a drinker. Unhappy marriage. After Bertie was gone, she climbed into the bottle and pulled it in after her. She wound up in St. Tropez. She took out her Ferrari and ran it into a palm tree. It was an accident.'

'Presumably.'

'But, Marvia — what was the story all about? I mean, if Vansittart was a confirmed bachelor, then why the fairytale about a wife and a son and the football team and the car crash in St. Tropez?'

Marvia said, 'I don't know. I'll get in touch with Willie Fergus, and with Placer County. We'll see what happens. They might even ask somebody at this end to look into it. Somebody will have to go down to Belmont and check out Vansittart's situation. Check those college records, too. See if there ever was a missus and a junior. If that happens, guess who gets the call.'

Later, they got into the Mustang and drove to Oxford Street.

★ ★ ★

Marvia was up and about long before Lindsey woke up; he'd enjoyed his introduction to sake, the Japanese rice wine, a little too much. He opened his eyes and saw that Marvia was scrubbing his face with a rough washcloth soaked in warm water.

'You tied one on, Bart. I've never seen you do that before. How's your head this morning?'

He sat up gingerly and put his hands to his temples. 'I'm okay.'

Marvia handed him a towel to dry his face. 'Do you remember what you told me about Vansittart, Junior?'

'Sure. Roger Cooke's cock-and-bull story.'

161

'While you were snuggled in the arms of Morpheus, I've been doing my job. Checked with the Santa Clara Sheriff's Department, Belmont Police Department, Hall of Records down there — nothing. Nothing on any missus or any junior. The late Mr. Vansittart was what CNN says he was, a lifelong bachelor. So, why the yarn?'

'Do you have any coffee, Marvia?'

'Sure, it's all made. I'll fix you a cup. But don't think this is the way it's going to be.' She handed him a cup of Jamaican Blue Mountain.

Lindsey gathered his thoughts. 'Mr. and Mrs. Cooke run the World Fund for Indigent Artists. The fund stands to collect four million smackers from International Surety if I can't turn up the woman on the cover of *Death in the Ditch.*'

'Have you found her?'

'No, but I've made some progress. I still think there's a chance.'

'What's their operation like? Are your friends the Cookes ragged-sleeve do-gooders? They operate out of a grimy walkup in the Mission? They are in San Francisco, right?'

'*San Francisco, sí, Mission, no.* They're in 101 California.' Lindsey described his ritzy luncheon date. 'Cooke picked up the tab, but he did it with a World Fund credit card. Showed it to me. They have custom cards; I guess they send 'em to their members. Every time you charge something on it, the fund gets a little rake-off.'

'So what this sounds like is, the Cookes are both old San Francisco money.'

'I think so. I don't think he worked his way through Stanford raking leaves. I didn't get as much from her, but I got a definite feeling. If she wasn't to the manor born I'll eat my hat.'

'Sounds to me as if they're doing well by doing good — if they're doing very much good at all. I think I'll send a telex to Sacramento and see if the fund is up on its filings. Be interesting to see what their annual revenue looks like, and what percentage of it gets used up on overhead. Want to bet that hardly any money actually gets into the hands of

down-and-out ex-cartoonists or whatever?'

'No bet.'

'Will you lock up when you leave here?'
Marvia asked him. 'I have to get to work.'

★   ★   ★

Kari Fielding smiled her adder's smile
when Lindsey arrived at the I.S. office in
Walnut Creek. He felt her eyes on his
back as he made his way to his desk and
picked up the memo slip. Just two words
were scrawled on it, in Kari Fielding's
favorite purple felt-marker ink. *Call
Richelieu.*

Mrs. Blomquist put him through to
Richelieu without keeping him on hold
for the usual five minutes. Richelieu
opened the conversation with a compli-
ment. 'You've been keeping KlameNet/
Plus up to date pretty well on this
Vansittart thing.'

Lindsey grunted an acknowledgment.

'I want that woman,' Richelieu said.
Ah, no more Mr. Nice Guy. 'You've been
running around like a chicken without a

164

head. What's your game plan now?'

'Is it all right if I call you back in five minutes, Mr. Richelieu?' Lindsey didn't wait for an answer. He hung up and walked out of the office, past a disbelieving Kari Fielding. He didn't like being the subject of her surveillance.

He called back on a public phone and got through to SPUDS/Denver. Richelieu was raging, but Lindsey managed to calm him down. 'There was somebody in the office — I didn't want to discuss internal matters. I've got a lead on the artist who painted covers for Paige Publications. If I can track him down, I think I might be able to find his model, or at least get a lead on her.'

He heard Richelieu exhale loudly. 'Okay, Sherlock. Keep at it. But watch your expenses. And remember, the clock is ticking. And don't hang up yet. What about the World Fund for Indigent Artists? You smoothing their feathers for them, or we going to have a lawsuit on our hands?'

'It doesn't look so good on that front, Mr. Richelieu. I had a meeting with Mr.

and Mrs. Cooke and they want the four million. They know about *Death in the Ditch* and they don't think there's any way we're going to find the model, so they're demanding the money. I think they're going to sue I.S.'

'Just try not to rile them. And see if you can find that woman. She's a million-dollar lady, Lindsey. Keep that in mind. You find her, you're a hero around here. You fail and . . . I don't like failure. Need I say more?'

Lindsey said no more. He knew if he held his silence, Richelieu would tell him something else.

'One other thing, Lindsey — have you seen the media coverage on the Vansittart case?' Lindsey heard Desmond Richelieu draw a hissing breath. 'We've been getting a rash of claims in the Vansittart case.'

'You mean besides the World Fund?'

'It's the wackiest thing since the Howard Hughes will mess. We must have had twenty women claiming to be the one on the cover of *Death in the Ditch*. Mostly the branch offices have been sifting these things. The messier ones get bucked to SPUDS. Find the rightful bennie, Lindsey, or at least find out what happened to her. Otherwise I've got a nice cozy desk for you to fly in Fargo, North Dakota.'

★ ★ ★

Lindsey phoned Shady Oaks Retirement Villas and arranged to take Jeb Harkins out for another dinner. He drove to the same restaurant where he and Harkins had eaten before. The place was pretty quiet tonight. They found a table and the same waitress approached.

Jeb Harkins said, 'I'll have my usual, señorita. You remember — whiskey sour?'

The waitress said, '*Sí, señor,* un wheeskee sour. And what for the *señor?*'

'Just mineral water, please.'

'*Sí, señores.*' She flowed away.

When their drinks came, they ordered dinner. Lindsey got ready to watch Harkins wolf it down. 'I hope you can give me a little more information about Bob Brown,' he said, 'the artist who painted the cover for your book, *Baseball*

Stars of 1952. Whatever became of him?'

Harkins shrugged, his jaw working steadily up and down.

'Do you know if he's still living in Chicago? Is he still living at all?'

Harkins swallowed and washed the *bistic* down with a swallow of whiskey sour.

'Did Brown ever say anything about his model? You told me you barely knew him, but I want you to try. Where did you meet? Did he come to the *Daily News* building or did you go to his studio?'

Harkins was following the waitress with his eyes. Now he brought them back to bear on Lindsey. 'Actually, he came to the paper to talk to me a couple of times, then I went over to his studio once to look at his painting. He was a bear when it came to anybody criticizing his work, but he wanted it to be accurate.'

'You went to his studio?'

'Old loft over on Talman Street near Douglas Park. He had an army cot and a primus stove; lived there and did his painting. I saw the original for my book.

He had everything right. I asked him about that weird ballpark. I told you about that, didn't I? Pelican Stadium, in New Orleans. He told me he used to be a hobo back during the Depression. Used to travel around the country, ride the rails, take odd jobs.'

He stopped talking long enough to sample his second whiskey sour. 'Used to get odd jobs as a groundskeeper and janitor. He told me he sold poor boy sandwiches in the stands at Pelican Stadium. Said that was his favorite town, New Orleans. If he ever retired he'd like to live there and paint.'

'When did Brown give up being a hobo?'

'Thirty-six, he told me. Civil war in Spain. Hated Hitler. Name like Bruninski, you can understand why, can't you? I never met him 'til '51, you see. But he told me he met a recruiter riding the rails in '36, talked him into volunteering, and off he went to Spain. Soldiered there for about a year, I think.'

'Did you ever see him after 1952?'

'Nup.'

'Ever hear from him — a postcard, anything?'

Harkins frowned. 'Let me remember.' He scooped up some rice and beans, then nodded. 'Think I got a Christmas card one year. Around the time Lyndon Johnson and Barry Goldwater were running for president. I remember, it was peculiar — he must have sent that card in October, because I remember getting it before the election. Just a Christmas card, but he must have sent it around Halloween. And they both signed it — Ben and Mae.'

'Who's Mae?'

'His wife. She was his model, didn't I tell you that? That time I went over to his studio to check the baseball cover for my book. He had the cover all done. It was right; had the right cap on Stan Musial and all. But he was painting a nude when I got there. He liked to do fine art — what he called fine art, anyway.'

He took another bite of burrito and washed it down with his whiskey sour. He frowned at the empty glass.

Lindsey signaled the waitress. Harkins

was a treasure trove. At their first dinner he'd denied knowing anything about Bruninski except his name. Now Harkins was revealing everything Lindsey had hoped for. Some door of memory had opened in the old man's mind. If only it stayed open!

'You say the model was his wife? Did he introduce you?'

Harkins' eyes looked far away. 'I tell you, Sunny Jim, that was the most beautiful woman I have ever seen. And I've seen a lot of 'em, believe me, and no disrespect to a one of 'em. They're all beautiful. Best damned thing God ever did, created woman.'

'Did she model for his book covers as well? Do you know her last name?'

'Never saw her again but that once. Lovely, lovely lady. Long hair, sort of a dark red color. Green eyes. You'd think, naked as a jay bird, you wouldn't exactly notice the hair and eyes. But I tell you, Sunny Jim, just one sight of that woman, you'd never forget a thing.'

'What became of Bruninski's work?' Lindsey asked. 'I mean, he sold it to

Paige, but that was just the publication rights, yes? What became of the original paintings?'

Harkins chewed for a while, then washed the food down with a swig from his glass. 'He was serious about his work, he was. Always meant to keep his originals and have an exhibition one day. Thought some gallery would give him a one-man show, or a museum would give him an exhibition. Bennie used to complain about those cheapskate publishers. Said they always wanted to keep the originals. He'd never let 'em do it. Demanded his originals back — and got 'em. Least he told me he did.'

'So you think he might still have the paintings? I mean, if he's still alive, and we could find him?'

Harkins shook his head. 'Not likely. He was always broke. He'd make a few bucks, then he'd get onto his uppers again. Whenever he got desperate, he'd sell off an original. They were good paintings, too. He could get some fair prices, but they didn't pay the kind of price for those commercial paintings that they would for abstracts. Not back then. Nobody wanted pictures that actually *looked* like anything. But he always found somebody who'd give him a few bucks for one, 'cause they were so good.' He paused for another bite of burrito and another sip of whiskey sour. 'That was all a long time ago.' He sighed. 'They were wonderful people, Ben and Mae.'

For someone who hardly knew Ben Bruninski and who only met his wife and model once, Harkins seemed to fall in love easily. Still . . . 'What happened to them?' Lindsey asked. 'When did they leave Chicago? Do you remember the postmark on the Christmas card they sent you in 1964?'

Harkins shook his head. 'No. But I remember the picture. Funny subject for a Christmas card. It was a statue of Andrew Jackson rearing up on a horse in a park.'

Lindsey knew the statue and the park. Jackson Square, New Orleans, home of Benjamin Bruninski's favorite baseball field, Pelican Stadium. Were they both still alive? In New Orleans?

'One other thing,' Harkins was saying. 'That Bob Brown, he was some character. Big, rangy galoot. A long drink of water, we used to say. Must have been six-five, six-six. Thin, stringy guy. Wore a little mustache and a goatee and a little blue beret. Had to prove he was an artist, see?'

Harkins shook his head. 'Bob Brown, he was easy to remember. Walked with a limp, too. At first I thought he was faking it — those arty types'll do anything for a little extra attention. But the day I went to his studio it was raining hard, and he was in real pain. He said he had some shrapnel in his leg, and it always hurt him when it rained. He was an interesting fella.'

He took a sip of his drink, then resumed. 'That gal Mae . . . believe you me, sonny, she was the most beautiful woman in the world.'

11

When Lindsey got home, there was a message for him to ring Marvia. She answered on the first ring, and didn't waste time on any preliminaries. 'O'Farrell's dead.'

Lindsey closed his eyes, shocked. He sank into an easy chair. 'What happened?'

'I had a call from Willie Fergus. He drove back up to Tahoe to join the search. They had the Highway Patrol alerted in both states, even sent up helicopters. Still nothing.'

Lindsey opened his eyes.

'Then somebody phoned in a fire alert. Claimed they saw a plume of smoke near I-80 west of Donner Pass. Forest Service totally freaked out. This isn't fire season, and they couldn't figure out why there should be a plume. So they sent a truck and they found it. That mysterious station wagon — it was a Jeep Grand Wagoneer. Stolen, of course. Ran off the freeway, over a ravine. They must have avoided the agricultural checkpoint at Truckee; that's easy enough to do. They got onto 1-80 for a few miles, then off again.'

'How do they know he's dead?'

'Wagon crashed and burned. A real mess. Gas tank must have been full. Highway Patrol wants to get into the act and the sheriff is all in favor. They think there might have been an explosive charge in the wagon. Just to make sure.'

'If the station wagon was that badly damaged, would the body be identifiable? Are they sure it's him?'

'No question. The body was thrown clear when the Wagoneer blew. They had to search to find him. It was O'Farrell, all right. Willie Fergus confirmed it.'

'He wasn't driving, was he?' Lindsey asked. 'Somebody arrived at Doctors' Hospital, O'Farrell checked himself out and they drove off together, right? So — where's the driver? You think those forestry guys or the Highway Patrol ought to search some more?'

'There were two sets of tire tracks leading off the freeway. Two leading off, one leading back. That makes a nice clear scenario. The whole thing was planned. Whoever was driving the station wagon knew that a confederate was going to pick him up along the way, follow him until he went off the freeway, and then pick him up in the second car once he'd disposed of O'Farrell. Or the pickup car might have got there first and waited for the station wagon.'

'What killed O'Farrell? The explosion?'

'Not sure yet, but it looks like a bullet in the brain. The M.E. up there has to let the sheriff know. They're keeping us posted.'

Lindsey stood up and paced back and forth. 'The guy goes from hero to suspect to corpse before you can blink your eyes! What now? Can't they take, what do you call it, a *moulage* of the second set of tire tracks? Trace the car from that?'

Marvia managed a small laugh. 'You've been reading too many murder mysteries, Bart. Right, CHP is trying exactly that, but they're not likely to get anything useful out of it. I mean, there are seventy-five zillion kinds of tires out there. Makes a nice story, but it won't work.'

Lindsey stopped pacing and checked his watch. Almost midnight.

Marvia said, 'Look, if you want to stay up to date on this, why don't you just watch some TV news? They're sure to have it by now.'

'Will do.' Lindsey picked up a remote and clicked to CNN. An advert was running; he hit the mute button.

'You learning anything useful, Bart?'

Lindsey said he was indeed. He'd put in a good night's work with Jeb Harkins. But then the commercial ended and the news at midnight came on. There was a still frame from Jamie Wilkerson's helicopter crash tape vignetted in a corner of the screen. The anchor was talking about John O'Farrell. Lindsey said, 'Marvia, I think I'm going out of town again. I'll call you in the morning, okay?'

The video report contained the same information Marvia had given to Lindsey, only in greater detail. The grandees at the network had rented a chopper of their own and sent it over the Sierras. It

178

hovered over the crash site and a camera with a long lens showed the CHP and CDF searchers carrying a body-bag away from the smoldering wreckage of a Jeep Grand Wagoneer.

When they seemed to be rehashing the same report rather than adding new facts, Lindsey turned off the TV and went to bed, and at length fell asleep.

He woke to pitch darkness, and blinked and fumbled until he located the bedside alarm. He must have flailed his arms in his sleep, because the clock-radio was turned away from his bed. He turned it back and read the glowing digital numbers. It had barely been an hour, but the harder he tried to go back to sleep the more awake he became. Finally he pulled on a set of sweats Marvia had given him, and a pair of sneakers.

The air outside was bracing. He decided to jog around the block. Marvia was always after him to get in shape. That was the reason for the sweatsuit.

He reached Hawthorne Drive and turned toward Palmer, keeping to the side of the road. There was no traffic at this hour, but caution was a habit. Most of the houses were dark, though light shone in an occasional window. Here was a row of hedges, here were a few trees, here was a driveway leading up to a square California craftsman home.

The car approached Lindsey from behind, its headlamps low. He heard it first, then turned and saw it moving slowly toward him. He wasn't sure what it was — certainly a recent model, and not an economy car, that was for sure. A Lexus or a Volvo or a Mercedes. This had to be some resident returning from a party or from an evening out in San Francisco. Yet something wasn't right.

The car pulled up alongside Lindsey. The passenger side window slid open with a soft hiss. He saw only a vague figure inside. A voice said, 'Pardon me, we've been driving around for an hour, completely lost. Do you — '

Something made Lindsey dive for the hedges lining the street. He managed to force his way through the vegetation. He felt leaves and thorns scraping his face and hands, but he pushed ahead and burst through onto a lush lawn. He sprang to his feet and sprinted toward the house.

Behind him he heard the same voice. 'Hey, wait — ' Then there were shots. He turned back. He could see the street, partly through the hedges and partly over them. The driver had turned on his brights, and a second car had rolled up Hawthorn behind the first.

There was another burst of gunfire. Lindsey heard a crash of shattering glass. Then the first car roared away toward Mountain View Boulevard. Unless there was a lucky traffic stop, Lindsey knew the car would be on Mountain View Boulevard inside sixty seconds, on the freeway and gone in a couple of minutes.

Lights were springing on in houses all around him. The second car had come to a halt in the middle of Hawthorne Drive. Lindsey trotted back to the street and stood in the glare of the second car's headlights. He heard the driver get out, and recognized him when he joined Lindsey in the glow of the car's lights. It was Gordon Sloane.

Sloane and Lindsey walked to the passenger side of the car. Mother had rolled down her window. 'Hobart, what happened?'

Lindsey said, 'I think we'd better call the police.'

The front door of the California craftsman house opened. The man who stood there wore pajamas and a robe. He held a very large revolver in his hand and was pointing it at Lindsey. 'Don't move.'

'Don't worry. Did you see — look, somebody just took some shots at me.'

The man peered at Lindsey. 'I know you.'

'I live nearby. Hobart Lindsey. Laurel Drive.'

The man lowered the revolver. A woman had appeared behind him, peering around him as if he were her barricade against all harm.

'What happened?' The man slipped the gun into the pocket of his robe. He caught sight of Sloane and Lindsey's mother as they came up. 'All right. Come on in.' He turned to his wife. 'Call 911, would you, dear?' They filed into the house and waited.

The police were fast. There were two of them, one male and one female, decked out in shiny midnight-blue nylon jackets with fake-fur collars. They had their hands on their pistols when they got out of the black-and-white.

* * *

The civilians sat in the living room with the female officer, her radio squawking every few seconds. She took quick statements from everyone present while her partner checked outside the house.

The officer radioed in Lindsey's minimal description of the first car. She told them that the police would try and stop any car roaring out of the neighborhood, but the one they wanted was probably gone already.

Once she had taken Lindsey's statement about the shooting, the officer took shorter ones from the others in the room. Then she started background questions. Did Lindsey recognize the car (no), did he recognize the person who spoke to him (no), did he have any enemies (in his line of work, who could tell), was there any known drug dealing in this neighborhood (not that he was aware of), was there gang activity in the neighborhood (not that he was aware of). The officer came back to that question about enemies. He told her about International Surety and about SPUDS.

'You look upset,' she said. 'I don't blame you, after what happened to you. But please don't hold back anything from me, however trivial.'

'Okay,' Lindsey said. Then he told her about ben Zinowicz, about Dave Jones the parole officer, and about ben Zinowicz's job with the World Fund for Indigent Artists.

'Have you seen this man since his release? Spoken to him?'

'No. but I've spoken with the directors of the fund. My company may have to pay the fund a great deal of money. And . . . ' He left it there.

'Why is that, sir?'

He explained about the Vansittart

insurance policy and the death of John Frederick O'Farrell.

She said, 'I've heard of that. Sensational case. You're involved?'

Lindsey felt like a celebrity. 'I work for the Special Projects Unit of International Surety. If I can locate the primary beneficiary of Vansittart's policy and we pay her the money, the fund gets nothing. Otherwise, they get four million dollars.'

The officer took a deep breath. 'And you think the directors of this fund are using this onetime professor, this . . . ' She checked the name on her pad. ' . . . this Nathan ben Zinowicz, as a hit man. He came here tonight looking for you. He was in your house once before, years ago, so he knows the neighborhood at least a little, and he was circling the block and saw you out jogging.' She gave Lindsey an inquiring look. 'Is that your scenario, sir?'

'Yes. That's it.'

The officer snapped her pad shut. 'In the morning we'll ask you to come down to headquarters and make a formal statement. But this should do for now.'

'Are you going to check with Dave Jones? With the fund office? With the Cookes?'

'We check everything, sir. Thank you.'

She went outside to check on her partner. Lindsey decided that the partner was included in everything. He entered the house and the two officers stood, conferring. Then the male officer walked to the far wall of the room. He grunted and nodded. He stood staring at a black-ringed hole in the cream-painted plaster. 'We'll have to get this out. One round here; there are more outside. We should get some useful information.'

A few minutes later they were back in the living room. 'All right, everyone.' The female officer was obviously in charge. 'Sorry for everything that's happened. Try to get some sleep. And, Mr. Lindsey, I'll see you tomorrow, all right?'

'Sure.'

She handed him her card.

Lindsey got a ride home from Mother and Sloane. If the householders had an International Surety umbrella policy, they had nothing to worry about.

It wasn't Lindsey's best night, but he managed to get a few ragged periods of sleep. A few hours later he drove downtown and parked the blue Volvo near police headquarters. He found his way to the officer's desk and gave his statement again, this time into a tape recorder. He asked what came next.

'I already had a chat with Dave Jones in Oakland. He said that Dr. ben Zinowicz had been a model client since he got his walking papers from San Quentin. Jones phoned that World Fund office where Dr. ben Zinowicz works, and he was there, bright and early this morning. Didn't know anything about an incident last night. Offered to do anything he could to assist in the inquiry.' She looked at Lindsey with innocent eyes. 'What do you make of that?'

Lindsey felt his jaw clench. 'I make this,' he managed. 'They're in cahoots. That's what I make.'

'Well, you may be right. Dave Jones told me that he'd called through again and talked to a Mrs. Cooke. She's a big shot over there, right? Do you know these people?'

'Yes. Cynthia Cooke and her husband run the place.'

'Well, they had a staff meeting last night. Mrs. Cooke, Mr. Cooke, Dr. ben Zinowicz. He was there with them. They started with dinner after work; they ate at — ' She consulted a notepad. ' — Harry Denton's, Steuart Street. Very chichi. Maître d' can verify that. Then they adjourned to the Cookes' condo on Nob Hill and continued until the wee hours. In fact, the meeting ran so late that Dr. ben Zinowicz had to put up in the Cookes' spare room. Poor baby.'

Lindsey blinked. 'So there's nothing.'

'Nothing to go on. You think it was this fellow. He's got an alibi. We could ask Dave Jones to bring him in for a paraffin test, but if he's as smart as he seems to be you can bet he was wearing gloves. And he's surely got rid of them by now.'

There wasn't much more to say. Lindsey was intrigued by this officer's dual role. Last night she was in a rolling unit, responding to a 911 call. Today she was sitting at her desk acting like a detective. But she seemed competent in both capacities.

Within hours Lindsey found himself sitting in another client chair, facing another female police officer across a battered, cluttered desk. This time the officer was Marvia Plum, and today she was decked out in her full, official midnight-blue uniform. When Lindsey told her about the shooting on Hawthorne Drive, she dropped her other work and listened to a repetition of the night's events and of this morning's meeting with the Walnut Creek Police Department.

'Trouble is, Bart, I don't know if I can take a hand in Walnut Creek's case,' she said. 'If you're right, and it ties in with WFIA and the Vansittart and O'Farrell killings, then I have a little hook into it. Very little. Only because I'm providing the local liaison with Fabia Rabinowitz.'

'So you can't do anything?'

She didn't answer directly. 'You didn't recognize the car? License number, make, anything?'

'It was dark. It was a fairly big sedan. I think it was black, but it could have been dark blue or dark green. I think it was a Mercedes, but it could have been a big Buick or Chrysler. And I didn't see the license plates at all.'

'So how do you know it was ben Zinowicz and not some random event mugging — '

'Come on, Marvia. What's your boss's favorite saying?'

'Okay, you're right. 'Coincidences really do happen, but they make me very nervous.''

'That's right. I'm working on this case. The World Fund stands to make a lot of money if I fail. Nathan ben Zinowicz has a major grudge against me. And he's now executive director of the fund.'

'Well, you cost him his academic career and several years of his life. I'd say that could produce a grudge.'

Lindsey felt a wave of helplessness wash over him. 'Do you need the rest of it? Ben Zinowicz gets out of San Quentin, gets a job working for the Cookes, hears about Vansittart's death and the big insurance policy — '

'No. He was working for the Cookes *before* Vansittart bit the big one. How's this for a theory? These three sweeties knew each other before Nathan went away. They were waiting for him when he got back. They knew all about Vansittart's eccentrically worded insurance policy, they knew about his gambling habit and his preference in transportation. They suborned O'Farrell. He was to dispose of Vansittart, which he did, very successfully. He was then to disappear, probably with a large stash of cash, provided by the Cookes. How's that?'

'Give me some more.'

'Okay. Everything is going fine until the helicopter comes down. Instead of ditching smoothly in Lake Tahoe, the chopper has a rough touchdown and starts to sink. Along comes Captain MacKenzie of the *Tahoe Tailflipper* and gets a line on the chopper, but he can't hang on to it and the chopper flips over as it sinks. Instead of emerging safe and sound, O'Farrell breaks his leg in the chopper crash. He winds up in the hospital.'

'Go on.'

'This makes the Cookes very nervous. They dispatch ben Zinowicz to break O'Farrell out of the hospital, which he does, very successfully. But O'Farrell is now damaged goods. Risky goods. So — maybe the Cookes and ben Zinowicz worked this out in advance. Incidentally, CHP up in Placer County *did* get some nice *moulage* of the second set of car tracks. Must be at least a million cars in this state could have those tires, and surely the Cookes have changed tires since then.'

She waved away an errant thought. 'Okay, here's the plan. Ben Zinowicz heads up to Truckee in the Wagoneer, the Cookes follow in their Mercedes, ben Zinowicz busts O'Farrell out of the hospital. O'Farrell is getting antsier by the minute, the longer he stays in there. He's afraid they're going to catch on to him, he'll hear a knock on the door, and it'll be the sheriff with an arrest warrant. Instead, he sees this nice friendly professor type — whom he probably knows already; we can't be sure of that, but I'll bet you a popsicle it's so — and a chance to get the heck out of there. You see?'

'Okay.' Lindsey nodded. 'And then?'

'Then ben Zinowicz tells O'Farrell that they're headed for Brazil via SFO, shoots him in the head instead, and dumps the body and the Wagoneer both off I-80. You like?'

'Go on.'

'The Cookes pick up ben Zinowicz, drive sedately home to their cabin in the sky, and nobody is the wiser. If they need an alibi, they alibi each other, all one happy little family.'

'And Hawthorne Drive?'

'You know about that. You were there.'

'So — how about you pick 'em up and close the case?'

'It's all speculation, Bart. If I went to the DA's office with that, they'd offer me an insanity discharge. There's no evidence.'

'Then nothing happens?'

'Hey.' She put her hand on his sleeve. 'That's not the end of story by a long shot.'

'So — what do we do now?'

She leaned forward, took his face in both her hands, put her mouth to his ear. He felt her breath, warm and moist. She whispered softly.

12

As the Delta 757 lifted off from Oakland International, Lindsey settled into his seat as best he could. He had the window and he watched the city and San Francisco Bay shrink and fall away beneath the jet as it headed inland. He'd made this flight to New Orleans once before, when he was tracing the tangled roots of a tragedy-smitten family to their origins in the tiny Louisiana town of Reserve.

This time he was looking for a onetime commercial artist named Bob Brown, born Benjamin Bruninski, and his wife, Mae. He'd taken a cursory shot at locating Brown/Bruninski via directory assistance — a few quick inquiries to the New Orleans Police Department and the Orleans Parish Hall of Records — but he felt something pricking at his mind about this case.

He was pretty sure that Ben and Mae Brown had both been alive and living in

New Orleans in 1964. A postmark would have clinched it; but even without the postmark, Brown's inclusion of Pelican Stadium in his cover montage for *Baseball Stars of 1952* and the scene of Jackson Square on Ben and Mae's 1964 Christmas card were the best clues that Lindsey had to work with.

The 757 landed in Dallas, but Lindsey didn't bother to deplane and sample the canned air and deadening atmosphere of the airport. When the jet was airborne again, he used the in-flight telephone to call Marvia.

She told him that Roger Cooke, Cynthia Cooke, and Nathan ben Zinowicz had all checked out for both the O'Farrell killing and the shooting in Walnut Creek. They alibied each other. Fabia Rabinowitz's work on the video images of both the helicopter crash and the wreck on the bed of Lake Tahoe had proved conclusively that O'Farrell had killed his passenger.

'And Willie Fergus tells me that they're going to try and raise the chopper,' Marvia added. 'The feds are insisting on

196

it, and then the coroner can get to work on the body and find out for certain if it's Vansittart, so everybody will be happy.'

'Marvia, I wish you could have come along.'

'So do I, but it just wouldn't work. Meanwhile, I'm sure that Aurora will take good care of you.'

'Sure. But it won't be the same.'

'I hope not.' She laughed, and rang off.

Lindsey made another call.

'International Surety, Special Projects, can I help you?'

He asked for Aurora Delano.

'Hey, sure, I know you're coming. I'll meet you at the airport.

He told her the landing time.

Coming off the jetway, he spotted her in the midst of a crowd of casually dressed New Orleanians. Lindsey and Aurora Delano had been to SPUDS training school together, in Denver. Before transferring to SPUDS, she'd been assigned to International Surety's tiny outpost in Grant's Pass, Oregon. When Lindsey got to know her, however, he learned that she was originally from

New Orleans, and was eager to return there. Her chief reason: an abusive husband whose farewell present to her had been a broken arm.

Aurora Delano waved a placard in the air, but Lindsey didn't need it to recognize her. They rode into town in Aurora's Saab sedan. She said, 'I got you a room at the Monteleone, you'll like it. On Royal Street, right on the edge of the Quarter. Where's your significant other? I liked her. Nothing bad happened, I hope.'

'Nothing bad. She's stuck at her job, I'm stuck at mine.'

'That's the modern way.' She flashed him a smile. 'Want to stop for some food? I told the hotel you might be late; they're holding your room. International Surety commands.'

'Sure. I didn't eat much on the airplane.'

★ ★ ★

They ate at Tortorici's on Royal, not far from Lindsey's hotel. The food was superb. Over coffee and chicory, Aurora got down to business. 'Le Duc de Richelieu called me before you did, Bart. He's really got a bug up his rear end on this one. I've never seen him like this.'

'How much info did he give you?'

'The whole file. Sent it to me over KlameNet/Plus. You've been digging, haven't you?'

'All right, then. You know why and how the trail led me here. I figure there's a fifty-fifty chance that Mae Brown or Bruninski is still alive. Same for Bob Brown. But it's been thirty years since that last Christmas card to Jeb Harkins in Chicago.'

Aurora's dark eyes flashed. 'I know you've done all the obvious things like checking the New Orleans phone book and running a check with the local credit bureaus.'

'That doesn't prove anything. They might be using a different name or just keeping their heads down. Nobody could tell me why they dropped out of sight in Chicago back in the early '50s. But they might have taken new identities. It would have been a lot easier back then; the country wasn't all wired up yet.'

Aurora said, 'Okay. Anyway, you let me know what else you want by way of support on this thing. Ducky has the hots for it, and we're both positioned to make big points — or to lose big.'

Lindsey put the meal on his I.S. credit card. Outside the restaurant, the evening air was warm and heavy. The valet pulled Aurora's Saab to the curb, hopped out and held the door open for her. Lindsey and Aurora climbed in.

She drove the length of Royal Street and brought the Saab to a halt across the street from the Monteleone. 'How about a nightcap? Or you too wiped out from flying all day?'

Lindsey took a rain check. He walked through the old hotel's ornate lobby, paused and admired a gigantic antique clock, then let the elevator whisk him upstairs.

When he climbed into bed he was too jangled to sleep. He phoned Marvia Plum. She was at home and they exchanged news.

Roger Cooke and Cynthia Cooke

continued to alibi each other and ben Zinowicz for both the O'Farrell murder near Truckee and the abortive assassination attempt in Walnut Creek, but ben Zinowicz had turned up missing. The Cookes had said nothing about his disappearance, but Dave Jones had decided to pull a surprise visit on the professor. The rules of the parole game permitted that. Ben Zinowicz had taken a flat in a Berkeley low-rise. Jones checked out the building himself. The landlord reported that ben Zinowicz had been an ideal tenant: paid first and last months' rent in advance, left a cleaning deposit, never disrupted the building's tranquility. None of the other tenants could remember ever meeting him.

Jones entered ben Zinowicz's apartment. He had installed floor-to-ceiling bookshelves, an up-to-date sound system, and a desktop computer. The shelves were empty of books and there was no evidence of CDs, audio tapes, or vinyl. Jones looked around for disks or documents associated with the computer but there was nothing. He did find a file cabinet near the computer table, but it, too, was empty. No clothing in the closet, no bedding, no toiletries, no food in the tiny kitchen. It looked to Dave Jones as if ben Zinowicz had packed everything he could take with him and left.

Jones tried to contact ben Zinowicz at the World Fund for Indigent Artists. There he had got a run-around. Dr. ben Zinowicz was away from his desk, he was out of the office, he wasn't in today, he was expected soon but no one knew exactly when.

Finally Jones spoke with Cynthia Cooke. She invited him into her private office, closed the door, and told him that she and her husband were desperately worried about Dr. ben Zinowicz. He had been acting more and more nervous lately, jumpy and suspicious, even paranoid. He hadn't reported for work in days, and the Cookes were beside themselves. He'd been an ideal employee. They knew that he was a paroled convict, but they'd known him before his first brush with the law, they had always held him in the highest esteem, and they'd been shocked at his conviction. Once he'd come up for parole, they'd jumped at the chance to bring him into their operation. His credentials were outstanding and his performance had been superb. What could have happened?

What happened was that Dave Jones had revoked ben Zinowicz's parole, Marvia told Lindsey. But that was little more than a formality. Ben Zinowicz's face and information about him would go to police departments throughout the state, but unless an officer happened to come across him in the course of the day's work, ben Zinowicz might stay on the loose for years.

Once Jones had done the paperwork necessary to revoke ben Zinowicz's parole, he returned to ben Zinowicz's apartment and seized the computer. Ben Zinowicz might not have wiped the computer's hard disk before he left. Maybe a police technician could decipher the information on the disk, and something there might lead to the fugitive.

Lindsey laid the telephone down. Then he removed the Paige Publications books from his flight bag and spread them carefully on a desktop. He sorted through all the ones that had a female model on the cover. The hair color and the hair styling, the clothing and the poses, were all different. Sometimes she was a tough gun-moll, sometimes a Caribbean wench. But whatever the costume or pose, she was always the same woman.

She was — she had to be — Mae Bruninski.

He picked up *I Was a Lincoln Brigadier* by Bob Walters. On this one she was either a nurse or a female guerrilla warrior, it was difficult to tell. She wore a uniform of sorts, stained and torn to reveal her generous bosom. But of course. A barren hill rose in the background. A wounded soldier lay across her lap; bombs burst around them and a propeller-driven fighter plane dove at them. The nurse or guerrilla fighter clutched a pistol in her free hand, pointing at the diving airplane.

Lindsey settled comfortably onto his bed. He read the blurb on the back cover, then opened to the first page.

I remember exactly where I was when I signed up for the Abraham Lincoln Battalion of the International Brigades. It all happened a decade and half ago but I remember it all, and I am not ashamed. I am proud to say that I was a Lincoln Brigadier.

The headquarters of the Young Communist League in Brooklyn were on the second floor of a building at the corner of 65th and Bay Parkway in Bensonhurst. There was a pharmacy on the first floor and a there was a bowling alley in the basement. You could get everything you needed in one building: entertainment in the basement, a meal or a magazine to read in the pharmacy, and nourishment for your mind and your soul at the Young Communist League.

When Colonel Francisco Franco came back from Africa and sent his mercenary thugs into Spain, the world recoiled in horror. Every decent man and woman knew what was going on. This was a man who hated democracy. He was in the pockets of Adolf Hitler and Benito Mussolini and Pope Pius

XI. What an unholy trinity! And Francisco Franco was their handmaiden and loyal servant!

There were forty of us in the room. All young, all idealistic. We believed in democracy and social and economic justice. We weren't all communists. Some were party members, sure. But there were Trotskyites, liberals, anarchists — everybody who recognized the growing threat. There were a lot of Jews there, too. They knew what Hitler meant, and they knew that if he wasn't stopped now he'd have to be stopped later, and at even greater cost. There were Negroes there. They knew — one of them said to me, 'If that man gets the Jews, we will be next. We know that. We've got to stop him *now*.'

Hitler and Mussolini were helping Franco, but who was helping democracy in Spain? Juan Negrin, the prime minister, sent out a call for help. The world clamped an embargo on Spain. Leon Blum, a Jew himself, was afraid to provoke Hitler. Neville Chamberlain, that sniveling coward, dared not lift a finger. He learned better, later, to his regret. They all learned better, later.

What about our dear Franklin Delano Roosevelt? He put a Jew in the cabinet and everybody thought he was so fine and noble. But he was in the pocket of the Church. Joe Kennedy, that old bootlegger and womanizer, whispered his filthy guidance into Roosevelt's ear, and Roosevelt said, 'Oh, those poor Spanish Republicans,' and 'Oh, those nasty Nazis and fascists helping that nasty General Franco.'

That was after Franco promoted himself. Later he decided that 'General' wasn't exalted enough, and started calling himself 'Generalissimo'.

As for Roosevelt, sure, he cried crocodile tears for democracy in Spain. He said a lot of the right things. But would he lift a finger to help democracy? Would he let the bullets and the airplanes and the blankets and the medicine and the food that Spanish democracy needed to survive, be sent to the Loyalists?

Oh, there was an embargo. Oh, the

League of Nations wouldn't permit it. So the supplies piled up in New York and in Liverpool and in France, and the borders were closed and the ports were sealed and the Spanish people suffered and Spanish democracy died. Spanish democracy was murdered, and Roosevelt and Chamberlain and Leon Blum and Edouard Daladier stood by and wrung their hands and did nothing.

Only the Soviet Union tried to help. Only Josef Stalin sent machine guns and tanks and airplanes and cadre to try to help. Too little and too late, but the International Brigades fought proudly and well. We will never bow our heads and we will never forget what we tried to do.

Maybe the world will remember some day.

Somebody blew a horn outside and Lindsey blinked. He'd been drawn into the book. It was written without grace or polish, but its obvious passion had caught him up. He laid it aside. It had been a long day. He took a shower, brushed his teeth, and crawled into bed.

He picked up the remote and tried the TV. Flipping channels, he found recorded talk shows. Oprah had a panel of females who all claimed to be the rightful beneficiary of the Vansittart insurance policy. Lindsey watched in horror until he could take no more. He clicked around to a rival show — who also had a panel of Vansittart claimants. He switched off the TV and went back to *I Was a Lincoln Brigadier*.

Again he was drawn into the story and read several pages:

Just about then, a party organizer arrived. The news was full of the war in Spain in those days, and he asked who wanted to go to Spain to fight the fascists. I raised my hand and he gave me $10 and handed me a piece of paper. 'Go see this man in the morning,' he said to me. 'Keep this paper. Give it to him.' Then he looked around. I remember he had rust-colored hair, very curly, and freckles. He asked if anybody else wanted to go to Spain. There was a lot of stirring around and muttering but nobody else raised his hand. Then the party organizer left.

I looked at the paper. It was an address and it was signed with the party organizer's initials.

A few of the fellows came over and patted me on the back and said they were proud of me. After a while the place started clearing out.

The next morning I went to the address the party organizer gave me. It was a doctor's office in Greenpoint. The doctor looked at the slip of paper. So, you want to fight Hitler, do you?' he asked me. 'Why?'

I said I wanted to fight fascism. I wanted to work for democracy and social justice. And I was a Jew.

The doctor examined me. 'You look healthy enough. Do you have any bad habits? How much do you drink? How much do you smoke? Do you run around with loose women?'

I answered truthfully and he nodded and went to his desk. He sat down and wrote out another slip of paper and handed it to me, telling me to go there the following Monday morning and someone would take care of me.

I left his office and looked at the slip of paper. It had an address on it in Manhattan, down in Union Square, and the doctor's initials on the bottom. I went home and started to pack a few clothes. My mother came into my room and asked where I was going. I told her I was going to Spain to help the Spanish people.

My mother started to cry. She said I would be killed. And she wouldn't let me go. So I told her I was going to work in a factory in Madrid making rifles. I would be perfectly safe, replacing a Spanish comrade so he could go to the front. Then she let me go.

Lindsey read until his eyelids drooped. He laid the book on the floor beside his bed and fell into a half-sleep.

He woke in a sweat. He went to the window, opened it, and looked out at the still-partying celebrants in the French Quarter.

'Toto,' he whispered to himself, 'I don't think we're in Chicago anymore.'

13

In the morning Lindsey started his search for Ben and Mae Bruninski. With Aurora Delano's assistance he looked for them through telephone books, old city directories, and back issues of the *New Orleans Times-Picayune*. Those were easy enough. Bank records were harder to come by, but Aurora had been running the local SPUDS operation long enough to have her contacts.

Together, he and Aurora turned up just three Bruninskis — Morris, Joseph, and Abraham. Morris was a retired florist in Metairie; he'd never been in Chicago, and had never heard of Benjamin.

Joseph was a lawyer. He was cagey but interested. Lindsey made an appointment to meet him at his office on Carondelet Street. He was too eager to ask questions and to listen, and too reticent on giving out answers.

Their face-to-face encounter justified

Lindsey's misgivings. Bruninski played the conversation like a poker wizard playing his hand. After a period of probing, Lindsey realized he was getting nowhere.

'Let's show our cards, Mr. Bruninski. Do you have any knowledge of a Benjamin Bruninski?'

By now Joseph Bruninski knew there was a lot of money at stake, and he knew that Lindsey was the party dispensing it. 'All right. Is this Benjamin Bruninski the beneficiary of an insurance settlement? If he is, and you involve me in the case, I'm entitled to be compensated.'

'No,' Lindsey told him, 'Benjamin is not the beneficiary. But I think I might find the beneficiary through him.' Lindsey was beginning to lose patience.

'You know,' Joseph Bruninski mused, 'I think I recall a Benny at family gatherings.' He frowned. 'Was he . . . uh, I'm trying to remember now. Maybe I'm thinking of Cousin Billy . . . '

This one should have been a palm reader, Lindsey thought. Looking for leads, picking up clues, trying to get him to fill in the blanks. He stood up. 'Thank you very much. I'm afraid I have another appointment.' And he got out of there

Abraham Bruninski was the chief rabbi of Temple Sinai on St. Charles Avenue. He welcomed Lindsey into his book-lined study. A framed painting hung on one wall, which showed a white-bearded scholar poring over what had to be a religious scroll. An oil lamp cast a golden light over the scene. The only other religious symbol in the room was a large menorah on a credenza.

The rabbi leaned back in his leather swivel chair. He wore a dark blue suit and maroon tie. When he heard what Lindsey wanted, he smiled. 'It happens that family genealogy is a hobby of mine.' He reached back and drew a large leather-bound volume from a shelf. 'You say this Benjamin Bruninski was a painter? Did book covers in Chicago, did he? That's interesting. I dabble a little myself.' He moved his head to indicate the picture of the pious scholar. 'Benjamin. Let me see . . . Here's Benjamin, all right. But he doesn't seem to be the right Benjamin.'

He laid the leather-bound book flat on the desk and turned it so Lindsey could read it. The rabbi pointed to an entry.

Bruninski, Benjamin, b. 1 Adar I, 5676 to Israel Bruninski and Vera Chemsky Bruninski, Brooklyn, New York. Unmarried, no issue, d. 6 Adar II, 5698, Belchite, Spain.

'You see?' The rabbi swung the book around again, closed it carefully and replaced it on the shelf. 'Benjamin Bruninski has been dead for more than fifty years.'

'I don't see. What were those dates, 5676, 5698? Are those from *Star Trek*?'

'Oh, excuse me, those are according to the Hebrew calendar. By our common calendar, Benjamin Bruninski was born on 5 February 1916 and died 9 March 1938.'

'Are you sure?' Lindsey didn't want to give him up.

The rabbi tented his fingers. 'What do you know about the Spanish Civil War, Mr. Lindsey?'

'Not much, but I've just been reading a book about the war. It's part of why I'm here. It happens that the cover was painted by a Bob Brown.'

'Oh?'

'Brown did some book covers, and I've located the author of one of the books. He knew Brown, and gave him some information to help make the picture accurate. He told me that Brown's real name was Benjamin Bruninski.'

'Now that sounds like a great detective story, Mr. Lindsey. But my research is pretty conclusive. Ever since the Soviet Union collapsed, records about that war that had been sealed since 1938 have been coming out. I visited Moscow personally to see what I could learn. Benjamin Bruninski is dead. His grave is in the Valley of the Fallen in Spain.'

Lindsey took a breath. 'Could there be a Benjamin Bruninski, Junior?'

The rabbi smiled. 'Our tradition is that the Word is sacred. The soul is tied up with the name. If a child were given the name of a living Jew, you see, there would be two persons competing for that soul, and one would probably die.' He grinned broadly. 'Of course, we don't believe in that nowadays. We're modern. Scientific. But you won't find many Jews named Junior.'

'Rabbi,' Lindsey said, 'could there be another Benjamin Bruninski?'

'Quite possibly. But if there is, I don't have him in my book.'

Lindsey thanked the rabbi. He walked to the streetcar stop and waited for the next car to carry him back to Canal Street.

Had there been two Benjamin Bruninskis? Had one of them died in Spain and the other returned to America? Or had someone else died in Spain and been misidentified as Bruninski? Or had Bruninski really died, and someone else taken his identity?

The olive-green streetcar ground to a halt and Lindsey climbed on board and paid his fare. No solution to the puzzle was in sight.

The Browns were worse. Four hundred of them in New Orleans and surrounding areas. Almost sixty Robert or Bob or R. Browns.

Lindsey returned to the Monteleone. Just off the hotel lobby he stopped for a meal of crawfish and rice. On returning to his room, he powered up his palmtop and logged onto KlameNet/Plus. He updated the Vansittart file to reflect the data he'd received from Marvia Plum, as well as the information earlier provided by Fabia Rabinowitz and Willie Fergus. There was nothing new in the file from Aurora Delano, nor any further instructions from Desmond Richelieu.

He stretched out on his bed and read a few more pages of *I Was a Lincoln Brigadier*. The book was compelling. The Lincoln Brigadiers really believed in what they were doing. And they might have been right.

If Franco had been stopped in 1936–38, and if Hitler's and Mussolini's so-called volunteers had been sent home bloodied and humbled instead of triumphant, would Hitler have hesitated before he attacked Poland the following year?

His lawyer friend Eric Coffman would

know that too. Coffman was a modern and worldly man, a little bit like Rabbi Bruninski for all the difference in their physical presences; but Coffman, too, could become obsessed with the monstrous tragedies of human conduct.

The bedside telephone rang, startling Lindsey out of his reverie. It was Aurora Delano.

'Okay, here it is. I've been looking at death records, and the good news is, I can't find either Ben or Mae Bruninski. If they've died in the past thirty years, it wasn't in Orleans Parish. Thank heaven for little disks.'

'But that doesn't prove they're still alive.'

'Nope. They might have met their maker from some other launching pad. You know, negative evidence is still evidence.'

'Did you look under Robert Brown?'

She gave a breathy laugh. 'There's a whole army of Robert Browns. We can track those all down, look at the d-o-bs and d-o-ds and see if any of 'em look right. Do you have a birth date for *our* Robert Brown?'

'That I have. Wait a minute. Here it is. February 5, 1916.'

'Okay. I can use that and work over the Robert Browns, see if any of them list that as a date of birth. And a date of death later than — ?'

'1964.' That was the date of the greeting card Bruninski had sent to Jeb Harkins.

'Okay. This is a long shot. But if Bruninski died in Orleans Parish and his death was recorded under the name of Robert Brown, and if the d-o-b on the death certificate matches up . . . '

'Got it,' Lindsey muttered. 'You have any other ideas?'

'I'll give our local police one more try. I've got some friends. A little personal contact might get more out of 'em than your phone calls did. There might be an arrest record or incident report somewhere in the dark recesses of a disk file or backup tape.'

Lindsey yawned. 'Okay.' He hung up the telephone.

After a refreshing shower, he dressed again, more casually this time, and left the hotel. He walked a block on Iberville to Bourbon Street. The afternoon sun had sunk low and the air was heavy and moist. Bourbon Street was getting ready to move into high gear. Gaudily dressed tourists wandered up and down, drinks in hand. Packs of college students in backwards baseball caps cruised the Quarter, looking for a night's adventure. Hookers of every sex and persuasion advertised their services.

Lindsey walked into an air-conditioned shop that featured New Orleans T-shirts, funny hats, Mardi Gras posters and china ornaments. He stopped at a rack of postcards. There were photographs of local sites and musicians, cartoons of drunks and grossly fat women, and sketches of the city's architecture. His hand leaped toward a card as he felt a bolt of ice-cold electricity streak down his back. He carried the card to a bright fluorescent fixture. It was a drawing of General Jackson on his rearing horse. It was a familiar sight in the city, prominently displayed in the park at Jackson Square in the Quarter and featured on posters and postcards available in a hundred shops.

Lindsey turned the card over and read the brief caption that went with the picture. There was no credit to the artist. He turned the card over again and scanned it, centimeter by centimeter, until he found what he was looking for: the artist's monogram, worked into the textured pattern of the statue's pedestal.

BB. Bob Brown.

Benjamin Bruninski.

He went back to the rack and examined the cards that bore a stylistic resemblance to the one of General Jackson. He found a series of various buildings, and there was even one with a sketch of a ballpark on it. He recognized Pelican Stadium: the drawing looked like the one on *Baseball Stars of 1952*. He carried the cards to the cash register and asked the clerk if she knew where they came from and if she could provide any information; tell him anything about the artist. She gave Lindsey a blank look and told him the price of the cards.

He paid for the cards and carried them back onto Bourbon Street. Evening was approaching and the crowds were thickening. He fought his way through until he found the Hotel St. Marie and shoved his way inside. The cool and quiet of the hotel refreshed him. He walked to the lounge, sat alone at a table, and ordered a mineral water.

Lindsey studied the cards until he found the telltale *BB* on each, then turned them over and read the brief captions. The card with the picture of Pelican Stadium explained that the ballpark had been torn down in 1957. None of the cards credited an artist, but they all listed the publishing company, Janus Novelty Press, and they all had copyright notices, © 1972.

He sniffed like a lion on the trail of its dinner. Now Lindsey knew that Bruninski had still been working in New Orleans as late as 1972. The trail was getting fresher!

Lindsey found a telephone and directory and looked up Janus Novelty Press. It was after closing time and there was no answer when he rang. He jotted the information in his pocket organizer, then started back toward his table, letting his eyes study the faces of the other patrons. A male figure leaned against the bar, his back toward the room. Lindsey could tell that his hair was gray and neatly trimmed. His clothing looked expensive. The man turned, and for an instant he made eye contact with Lindsey. Horn-rimmed glasses, gray spade-shaped beard. Lindsey blinked. The man threw a bill on the mahogany and scurried from the room.

Lindsey dropped his package of postcards and ran after him, but the man plunged into a crowd of milling tourists. Once Lindsey thought he spotted the man's head bobbing above the crowd, but before Lindsey could close the distance he had disappeared.

Returning to the St. Marie, Lindsey retrieved his postcards. For the second time, he left the St. Marie. He ducked around a corner and walked the short block on Toulouse Street back to Royal.

Here, art galleries and antique shops competed for shoppers' dollars. They offered Lindsey welcome relief from the strip joints and trashy shops of Bourbon Street. He'd browsed through half a dozen shops before he froze in his tracks. He felt a touch on his arm. The individual who stood at his elbow had a decided proprietary air about him. He had black wavy hair that glistened with pomade, a neat mustache, and a pinstriped suit.

'Magnificent, isn't it?'

'Is it for sale?' Lindsey asked.

The proprietor smiled. 'But of course. Do you collect fine nudes, sir?'

'No, I — '

'I understand. This is a most unusual painting. We had it in the window for a few days, but we had to move it back here. People were blocking the sidewalk. It's really a bargain, but I must confess, I've been tempted to buy it for myself and take it home. It is unique, don't you think?'

'Unique.' That was the truth.

Lindsey would have bet everything he owned that he knew the artist and the model. He remembered what J.B. Harkins had said about Benjamin Bruninski's ambition; about how he tried to hold on to his originals but always wound up selling them off when he was broke. Lindsey asked the proprietor the artist's name. He handed Lindsey a business card.

B.D. 'Buddy' Peabody
Proprietor
Peabody Fine Art and Antiques
Royal Street
New Orleans, Louisiana.

In a fine hand, in purple ink, was a local telephone number.

Lindsey opened his pocket organizer and handed Peabody one of his own International Surety cards. Then he asked again the artist's name.

'Robert Brown.'

Lindsey didn't need to hear. He knew a Benjamin Bruninski when he saw one after studying those covers. And Lindsey knew who the model was. The background was the same hillside as that on the cover of *I Was a Lincoln Brigadier.* Lindsey couldn't spot the BB signature, but surely it was there. The wounded soldier was gone, as was Mae Bruninski's torn uniform. This was a portrait, *sans accoutrements*, of Mae Bruninski. The tiny airplane still dove, and Mae still pointed her pistol defiantly skyward. Without a doubt, Jeb Harkins had been right.

'Do you know when this was painted?'

'Approximately forty years ago. The artist brought it in himself. Doesn't work through an agent. I was very surprised. He'd held it off the market all these years, but I didn't doubt that it was painted much earlier in his life. And there are ways to tell from the condition of the paint and canvas. It has a title, by the way. Did you notice the placard? *La Pasionaria*. It's truly magnificent.'

Lindsey said he'd like to meet the artist, but Peabody refused to give out any information about him. 'He's a very private individual, sir. I promised him faithfully not to reveal his whereabouts to anyone. Besides, the policy of the gallery . . . I'm sure you'll understand.'

Lindsey studied the painting again. How had Bruninski got that color and that *life* into Mae's green eyes? And her skin — Lindsey could almost feel her heat and the sweat and the dirt on her skin. The painting was erotic, but it was more than that: it was political; it was about freedom and courage and idealism. It was amazing.

'Suppose someone bought the painting? Could the buyer meet Bob Brown?'

'Well, I would certainly convey your wishes to the artist. I can promise no more than that.' Peabody paused. 'But I expect he would be amenable. Yes. Would you like to put down a deposit, or would you care to pay the full amount now?'

'Wait. What's the price?'

Peabody held out his hand. Lindsey handed his card back to him. Peabody extracted a magnificent antique Waterman from his suit pocket and wrote a number on the back of the card and handed it back.

Lindsey read the number Peabody had written there in purple ink. He counted the number of zeroes after the number five.

'Is this price negotiable?'

'Alas,' Peabody sighed, 'the artist insisted that his price be met, and we take only the smallest markup to cover gallery overhead.' He shook his head regretfully.

Lindsey put Peabody's card in his pocket and left the gallery. He walked up Royal Street, looking in windows just on the off chance that he'd spot another Ben Bruninski original. He didn't really expect to see one, and he was not disappointed.

14

Lindsey didn't want to face Desmond Richelieu or encounter him by telephone, *viva voce*. Instead he put a message up on KlameNet/Plus. It was brief.

Need $50,000 to buy great nude painting. Wd be perfect for yr office. Might also save International Surety a cool million.

He connected the laptop to the hotel room telephone jack and zapped the message off to SPUDS headquarters. Then he climbed into bed, picked up *I Was a Lincoln Brigadier*, and studied the cover again. The original might have had some of the passion, some of the soul of the gallery nude, but clearly the nude was Benjamin Bruninski's masterpiece.

Lindsey opened the book and read.

I walked the rest of the way to the address I had been given. It was an unmarked party facility. A comrade

231

took me downtown to the Federal building and helped me apply for my passport. He warned me that my passport would be stamped *NOT GOOD FOR TRAVEL TO SPAIN.* When I filled out my application I would have to say that I was going somewhere else. I wrote on the application, '*Paris — student.*'

I was given money and sent to a war surplus store and told to buy a World War I uniform and helmet. With my bag and my uniform carefully packed in it and my passport in hand, I was given a third-class ticket to Le Havre and told that other volunteers would be on the boat, but I was not to recognize them and absolutely not to talk to them.

There must have been thirty or forty of us, and we recognized one another at once. All around us were bourgeois families on vacation, children from middle-class homes going to Europe for their cheap-jack version of the Grand Tour, and retired immigrants going back to see the old country again. And thirty or forty of us, young idealists, on our way to Spain.

All we talked about was the war. What was Franco up to? Could Juan Negrín and his government be trusted? Would Roosevelt lift the embargo? Could Stalin get enough help to the democratic side to stop Hitler and Mussolini from winning? The ship received war news by radiotelegraph, and a daily newspaper was published by mimeograph with a summary of world events. We crowded around it and discussed the events every day.

At Le Havre we were again met by a party representative and given third-class coach tickets on the train to Paris. From there we traveled by rail to the Spanish frontier, where we had to get off and sneak into Spain. We carried our baggage in our hands as we walked through the Pyrenees.

It wasn't a long walk. We set out at sunset, and by dawn we were in Spain. We had avoided the border guards, and we realized with a rush of exhilaration that we were really in Spain! We changed from our civilian clothes into our uniforms. Once more we were met by comrades, who fed us, put us on trucks, and sent us to the south.

Training was given to us by cadres sent by the Spanish people or their Soviet allies. They supplied us with rifles and ammunition, and taught how to use them. Then we were headed for our first engagement on the Aragon Front, the Battle of Belchite!

★ ★ ★

Upon awakening, Lindsey looked for a message on KlameNet/Plus. There was nothing. Next, he opened the telephone directory and looked up the publishing company that had produced the Bruninski postcards. To his relief, they were still in existence. He jotted the company's address in his pocket organizer, then studied a city map until he found the location of their office.

He left the hotel and walked down Royal Street, carrying his palmtop computer in a shoulder kit. He wanted to be able to reach KlameNet/Plus by modem from any telephone, not just from his room at the Monteleone. He reached Canal Street and climbed aboard a bus to Tchoupitoulas Street and found the address he was looking for.

Janus Novelty Press apparently consisted of two elderly brothers and a female office manager. Lindsey showed them the Bruninski cards he'd bought the previous night and the brothers confirmed that they had indeed published them. He asked if they could give him Bruninski's address.

The office manager rolled open a drawer in a sagging file cabinet, pulled out a battered manila folder, and laid it in front of the brothers. The older-looking brother opened the folder. There wasn't much in it. He whispered a few words to his brother, then told Lindsey, 'I remember this guy. Funny duck. He brought in his drawings. They were really good. Wanted to sell 'em to us. He wouldn't take any royalty deal; wouldn't take our check.'

The office manager chimed in. 'I

remember that guy. Wouldn't take nothing but cash. I told him he'd make a lot more money off royalties, but he only wanted cash.'

Lindsey asked if they had any address for the artist. The older brother looked in the folder and said, 'No, nothing. Look.' He shook the folder at Lindsey. A few pieces of paper fell out — a list of drawings, a statement, a receipt for cash. The signature on the receipt was an illegible scrawl.

No name, no address, no phone. Nothing. It was peculiar: the man's artistic ego still made him sign his work, but Bruninski himself stayed in hiding.

'Did he say anything about where he lived, how you could get in touch with him?'

'Nothing.'

The office manager said, 'I remember that funny geek. Tall, skinny, wore a little beard and a beret and walked with limp.'

'But that guy could really draw. We still use his stuff,' said the second brother.

Lindsey left his International Surety card with the office manager. On the back he wrote the name and address of his hotel, and the Monteleone's telephone number and his room. 'If you come across anything, or if you remember anything, give me a call, please. At the hotel, or if I'm not there, call the International Surety number. Call collect; this is important.'

Lindsey rode a bus back to the edge of the French Quarter. He stopped in a restaurant on Decatur Street and ordered a shrimp salad and a beer. A television above the bar was tuned to the weather channel. In the northeast a monster snowfall had shut down major cities from Boston to Baltimore. Closer by, a storm was brewing over the Gulf of Mexico, and it was feared that it might sweep inland and cause flooding in Louisiana and Mississippi.

He finished his food and drink, then located a telephone and tapped into KlameNet/Plus. There was no message for him. He tried the Monteleone switchboard, but they had nothing. Surely Richelieu had received his request by now?

He stepped back into the moist afternoon. Tourists were swarming into New Orleans, eager to escape the blizzard in the northeast. Musicians and mimes competed for coins. Sketch artists would provide instant charcoal portraits for visitors to take back home and show off. If you didn't fancy a picture of yourself, how about one of Elvis?

Lindsey joined a small group watching a sketch artist create a portrait of a young mother and her new baby. When picture had been exchanged for cash, Lindsey asked the sketch artist if he knew a Benjamin Bruninski or Bob Brown. He described him as best he knew.

The artist shook his head. Lindsey tried half a dozen sketch artists plying their trade around the square with the same negative result.

He phoned Aurora Delano at her office. She'd drawn a blank as well. Discouraged, he returned to his hotel room, where he took off his shoes and swung his feet up onto the bed. He picked up *I Was a Lincoln Brigadier* and opened to his bookmark. He found himself skimming the chapters, reading a few paragraphs here and a few pages there. Lindsey had a suspicion that he knew who the author was.

He came to a description of an engagement at the town of Quinto, south of the Ebro River:

We were pinned down. Our boys had fought well; we'd had our baptism of fire, and we knew what it was to see our comrades blown to bits by Franco's mercenaries.

Let me be clear about one thing. Whose side were the Spanish people on? Sure, some of Franco's soldiers were conscripts, boys with no political awareness. Some of them were good Catholics, and Franco told them that they were defending Holy Mother Church against the enemies of Christ. When we got our hands on them, we just sent them to the rear. They were disarmed and neutralized, and that was that.

The fascist officers were another story, though. And the rest of General

Franco's followers were colonial mercenaries from Morocco. They took their devil's shilling and they fought their master's battles. If they'd understood the true nature of colonialism, they would have turned on their masters and shown them the business end of their rifles — but they didn't understand.

Even the Germans and Italians were divided. Hitler and Mussolini sent their legions into Spain, but there were detachments of Germans on our side as well — *real* volunteers who knew what they were fighting for, not bully boys in the pockets of their swaggering bosses!

There was the Botkin Brigade — brave Jews from Poland whose eyesight was clear enough to show them what was coming if these bullies weren't stopped. The bullies could have been stopped in Spain, but they weren't — not in Spain, anyway — and the world lived to regret that mistake.

The fascists had more guns, more bullets, more tanks. But they were content for a while to let us sit there in our emplacements, waiting for what we knew had to come.

Then the Condor Legion arrived. German aviators, so-called Luftwaffe 'volunteers' commanded by Wolfram von Richthofen, some bastard scion or cousin or nephew of the famous Red Baron. They came in Focke-Wulfs and Messerschmitts, piloted by Herman Goering's pets, the same pets who would destroy Coventry and blast half of London from the map a few years later.

But we had airplanes, too! If Roosevelt had let us have some Thunderbolts and Warhawks, we could have matched those fascists, but Roosevelt was neutral. Neutral!

Stalin sent what he could. I remember once I saw a medium bomber, twin engines droning, heading out on some mission. One plane, alone. It never came back.

We had fighters. Ilyushin 15s and 16s. The 15 was an older model, a biplane that looked like something left over from the first war. We had plenty of those. We had a few of the 16s, too. The 16 was more modern, a single-engine monoplane. The Spanish people had even built an airplane factory, with Soviet help, and they were building their own Ilyushins, right there in Iberia.

But our Ilyushins still weren't up to the Condor Legion. We had good pilots. The Soviets had sent some of their best to help the Spanish Loyalists —Yakov Smushkevich, Pavel Rychagov, brave pilots and decent men.

But the Condors outnumbered us and outgunned us, and we could see the Ilyushins falling from the sky. Then one of our boys got a Focke-Wulf in his sights, and we saw the smoke pouring from its engine, then the plane go into a dive. The pilot parachuted out. I wish we'd caught him, but he landed on the other side of the Ebro River, behind the fascist lines.

Then, just when we thought the battle was over, the Heinkels came. They were old, slow biplanes. If only they'd come earlier, our boys could have knocked them down. It would have been a fair fight. But that was the whole idea, as we soon realized.

The Heinkels came in low and they started dropping bombs. *Flambos!* Get splattered by the flaming death that those things spewed out, and you didn't have a chance.

I was sitting behind a Maxim machine gun when one of those things landed near me. I was lucky I wasn't burned to death. The flambo sent dirt and rocks flying and one of them hit my ammunition box. The only reason I wasn't killed was my comrade, Mel Nance.

The Lincolns were the first American military unit where Negroes and whites fought side by side, as equals and as comrades. Mel caught most of the explosion. He was killed on the spot. I caught a piece of shrapnel in my leg. A major artery was severed and I would have bled to death if somebody hadn't slapped a tourniquet on me. I don't know to this day who it was, but I owe him my life.

I wound up in the hospital, and that was where I met the woman who was to become my partner for life.

Lindsey closed the book and lay staring at the ceiling. Harkins had been convinced that Ben Bruninski's limp was the result of a real injury. Harkins had met Bruninski's wife, Mae, who had served as the model for most of the Paige book covers. And Lindsey had seen Bruninski's painting, *La Pasionaria*, clearly modeled by the same woman who had posed for the cover of *I Was a Lincoln Brigadier*.

Eventually Lindsey fell asleep.

He awoke in a state of confusion. His room was dark, the sky outside was dark, and rain was falling in heavy sheets. The rumble of thunder and flashes of lightning punctuated the storm.

And his phone was ringing.

15

Lindsey padded to the window. He looked out toward the French Quarter and the Mississippi beyond. The predicted storm had arrived from the Gulf of Mexico more rapidly than anticipated. The sky was almost black, what little light there was scattered by thick storm clouds.

He looked down into Royal Street, dimly by rows of evenly spaced street lamps. A man was standing in the rain across the street, looking up at Lindsey's hotel. A flash of lightning illuminated the street and Lindsey got a brief, clear look at the man's face.

The sharp features, the thin cheeks, the gray spade-shaped beard, the angry eyes behind their horn-rimmed glasses. There was no question, then: it had been Nathan ben Zinowicz at the St. Marie.

An involuntary moan escaped from Lindsey's throat. When he looked down into Royal Street again, two figures ran by, arms around each other, sharing an umbrella. They disappeared in the direction of Canal Street. There was no sign of ben Zinowicz.

He picked up the phone and dialed Marvia Plum's apartment in Berkeley. Willie Fergus answered the phone.

Stammering, Lindsey identified himself. Fergus handed the phone to Marvia. She said, 'Bart, what is it?'

'He's here. I just saw him. Nathan ben Zinowicz. I saw him earlier and tried to catch him, but he disappeared in a crowd. He must have followed me. I was trying to follow him but I gave up. I guess he turned the tables on me. There's a storm now and I'm in my hotel. I was looking out the window, there was a flash of lightning, and he was standing in the street looking at my hotel.'

There was a moment of silence, then Marvia said, 'What did you do? When did this happen?'

'Just now.' Lindsey was standing at the window again, telephone in hand. 'When I looked again, there was no one to be seen. Then a couple ran by, arms around each other, sharing an umbrella. They vanished in the direction of Canal Street.'

'Bart, I don't mean to doubt your word, but are you certain it was him?'

'It *was* him. You told me that he skipped town. He killed John O'Farrell up in the Sierras and he tried to kill me in Walnut Creek. He's working for the Cookes. Now he's in New Orleans.'

'Bart, there's news from Tahoe. They got the body up. It's Vansittart, all right.'

Lindsey grunted.

'They haven't been able to get the helicopter, and they don't have the tire iron, but the body is his, and the hole in his skull — O'Farrell would be in hot water now if he were alive. But now I guess it's moot.'

'He wasn't acting on his own, Marvia.'

'Oh, you're right about that. We're working on that.' She was almost babbling, something Lindsey had never heard her do.

Lindsey tried to calm himself. He looked at the bedside clock and subtracted a couple of hours. 'All right, what do I do now? Marvia, I wanted you with me. I know you couldn't come, but I need your help. What do I do now?'

'I'll call Dave Jones first thing in the morning. I'll tell him that ben Zinowicz has been sighted in New Orleans. We'll widen that APB and we'll get in touch with the police in New Orleans.'

'Okay. Do you want me to call them?'

'No, we'll take care of it. Coming from another police agency, they'll take it more seriously.'

'Okay.' Lindsey was still agitated. 'Why is he here? What does he want?'

'I don't know, Bart. If he was really standing outside your hotel tonight — well, how did he know you're there, and what do you think he wants?'

'I don't — wait a minute! Scotty Anderson, the paperback collector who gave me my lead on Paige Publications and Chicago, told me that a guy called Lovisi — he publishes a collectors' journal — told him that somebody else was trying to track down information on Paige Publications. You know ben Zinowicz used to be a big-time academic; he knows how to do this kind of research. He was working for the Cookes and he heard about *Death in the Ditch*. He knows mass culture, right? He was involved with the old comic book case. He knows about paperbacks, too.'

'Go on.'

'He could have done the same work that I did; learned the same things that I did. Maybe he followed the same trail; maybe he found some other collector than Anderson, or turned up one of the other Paige authors. I don't know how he followed my trail to New Orleans, but he must have picked me up somehow, and now — I don't know what he's up to. Marvia, *I just don't know!*'

'All right, Bart. Look, we've had more news here from the computer people. That's why Willie Fergus is back in Berkeley; he came in from Reno to talk to the silicon wizards about ben Zinowicz's computer. They got some information off his hard disk. We were going to get the info to you anyhow, so let me put him on, all right?'

Lindsey stood holding the telephone,

watching the sheets of rain fall past his window.

'Mr. Lindsey? Sergeant Fergus here. These computer folks here in Berkeley ran some of their software on ben Zinowicz's computer, the one he left in that apartment. No wonder nobody ever saw him there. He used that place for a secret hideout. Anyhow, your good guys put in some kind of special programs for recovering deleted files, and they turned up plenty. You want to know what they found there?'

'I'm listening, Sergeant Fergus.'

'One of the things they found there was a list of books. Does this ring a bell? *Buccaneer Blades, By Studebaker Across America, Al Capone's Heirs* . . . '

'That's the Paige bibliography. Does he have *Death in the Ditch*?'

'It's here, Mr. Lindsey.'

'That does it. He's following the same trail that I am.'

'I'll talk it over with Sergeant Plum. We'll talk to Dave Jones, and we'll get the NOPD on it. They'll probably want to talk to you. Maybe you should check in with them before you leave your hotel in the morning. Is that all right, sir?'

'Right. Okay.'

'One more thing, then. Mr. Lindsey, did David Jones tell you how many parole violators we have out there?'

'Thousands.'

'That's right. No judge or police force there in Louisiana is going to peep if Dave Jones tells 'em that a parolee has left town without permission. So you better convince those New Orleans officers that this man represents a serious danger to others. Do you understand that, Mr. Lindsey?'

'I understand.' He hung up and returned to his bed.

He was awakened by the telephone and by a soft female voice asking him to come down to the French Quarter police station, if that wouldn't be too much trouble, and help the New Orleans Police Department straighten out a troublesome matter that they'd just been asked to look into. It was a short walk from his hotel. If he just said that he was Mr. Lindsey, an officer would be waiting to chat with him.

He got there as fast as he could. The storm had passed over the city, and the sky was blue, but it had left some damage in its wake. There was standing water in some of the streets, the surfaces of the temporary ponds broken by bits of vegetation and assorted detritus. And a number of shops and bistros had apparently had their plate-glass windows blown in or smashed by flying debris.

Lindsey's route took him past Peabody Fine Art and Antiques. The front window was gone, replaced by a sheet of plywood.

The police officer he talked to at the station was polite and sympathetic. He'd heard from Sergeant Plum in California, and he was eager to do anything he could to help.

'Can you find this guy?' Lindsey demanded. 'He's wanted for a parole violation at the very least.'

'I know that,' the officer said. He tapped a document with his finger. 'Trouble is, if we get a hold of him, he doesn't have to go back to California if he doesn't want to.'

'But it's more than parole. He probably

committed another murder and an attempted murder.'

The officer's eyebrows moved up. 'Nothing about that here. You know about these incidents?'

'I was the target of the attempt. He shot at me.'

'The police know about this in California?'

'Of course they do.'

The officer studied the paper once more, as if he hadn't read it before. 'Well, maybe we ought to check this fellow out. Where is he staying, sir?'

'How am I supposed to know that? I just looked out my window last night and there he was, watching my hotel.'

'I see.' The officer nodded. He didn't volunteer any further help.

'Well,' Lindsey said, 'what are you going to do?'

'What can we really do?' the officer asked. 'There are hundreds of hotels and motels and rooming houses in greater New Orleans. And if this fellow has any brains, it's very unlikely he's using his real name. And we can't just line everybody up and check their IDs. People have civil rights.'

Lindsey bit his lip. The officer gave him his card and suggested that he phone if he spotted ben Zinowicz again. 'Don't approach him, sir. Just phone me. If I'm not here, someone else will take the call.' That was that.

Back in his hotel room, Lindsey logged onto KlameNet/Plus. There was a message waiting for him from Desmond Richelieu in Denver.

With your shield or on it.

That, plus a series of digits that Lindsey recognized as an International Surety financial control number. He was authorized to spend the $50,000 for *La Pasionaria*. He knew now that he had Richelieu's backing. And he knew that if he failed, his career was on the line.

He keyed in a report on his activities and shot it off to Denver. Then he checked his wallet to make sure that he had his company charge card, left his hotel room, and started down Royal Street for the second time that morning.

Workers had already replaced the plate-glass window at Peabody Fine Art and Antiques. The store had taken some water damage, but altogether things were not in bad shape. Lindsey got a quick look at *La Pasionaria*. The painting was undamaged.

Peabody looked stressed. Lindsey told him that he wanted to discuss the Bruninski painting. He led Lindsey to a private office.

'I have to set a condition,' Lindsey said. 'If I make this purchase — '

'Is this for yourself, sir?'

Lindsey frowned. 'No. It's part of a corporate acquisition program. For my company.' He gave him the details.

'Ah, certainly.' Peabody had placed himself behind a massive, ornate desk. 'Many corporations are making such wise investments nowadays.'

'If we make this purchase, it's absolutely imperative that I meet the artist.'

Peabody's smile faded. 'We already discussed that, sir. I'll definitely try to arrange a meeting, but I can't promise you — '

'How soon can I meet him?' Lindsey was insistent.

'It may take a little while. You see, the storm . . . well, we'll have to back up our computer files. There was a little damage last night, and — '

'The storm destroyed your files?'

'Everything is backed up. We lock away our backups; they go into the safe every night, and to the bank vault once a week. We'll find the address.'

'You mean to tell me you don't know where the artist is, but you have his address in your backup files?'

'Sir, I cannot memorize the address of every person I do business with. Please, Mr. Lindsey, I'm afraid you're becoming agitated. There's no cause for alarm. I'll get the artist's address and contact him. I'm sure he'll be willing to meet with you, if that is a condition of the transaction. In the meanwhile, permit me to draw up a bill of sale.' He opened a drawer of his ornate desk and pulled out a book of blank forms. He started by asking Lindsey for his permanent address.

Lindsey didn't go for it. There was

something the matter here. Peabody was too eager to get a signature to close the deal.

He stood up and started for the door, then turned back. 'You find Bob Brown. You set up a meeting for me. Then we'll see about the $50,000.'

'Please, Mr. Lindsey! It's obvious to me that you are not an experienced art buyer. That would be a violation of professional ethics. We could never permit that.'

'All right. Thank you.'

Peabody was around his desk and tugging at Lindsey's sleeve. 'All right, I have to tell you something that happened last night. Please — won't you sit down again? This is a very difficult matter.'

Lindsey remained standing.

'We have a security system here, of course. We deal in expensive goods; we have to safeguard against break-ins. Last night when the front window was smashed the alarm went off. We contract with a private security service, and they respond when the alarm sounds. I arrived from my home, also, and the security people were already here.'

He paused and mopped his brow. 'We thought it was just the storm, you see. Nothing seemed to have been taken. We would have put up the plywood beforehand, but we had no inkling of how severe the storm was going to be. Well, this morning I checked the office, and our locked file had been broken into. We keep routine papers in unlocked files, you see; but anything to do with sources of merchandise or with customers, why, we regard those as sensitive files and we keep them in a locked cabinet.'

Lindsey watched a drop of perspiration fall from the tip of Peabody's nose.

'Mr. Brown's file was stolen. Just that one file.'

Lindsey felt as if a cold hand had wrapped itself around his chest and squeezed. Ben Zinowicz had to be the person who had stolen Bruninski's file from Peabody.

'But we really do have computer backups. We'll recover the address. I can have it for you today. Really.'

Lindsey said, 'Call me at my hotel. I'm

at the Monteleone. Call me when you have the file.'

He left Peabody behind, flapping his hands and gasping for air.

16

Lindsey circulated through the French Quarter. If Bruninski was still in New Orleans, it made sense that he would be known by other artists in the city. If you were looking for an alcoholic, there was a good chance you'd find him in a bar. And an artist would stay with other artists.

Lindsey found Benjamin Bruninski on the corner of St. Peter and Chartres. He'd tramped the Quarter for hours, hoping against hope to find the man. Now it was nearly sundown.

It was the music that first attracted Lindsey's attention. New Orleans was full of music, most of it jazz; but this was no jazz tune, and it was coming from a boom box. It caught Lindsey's attention, and he recognized the melody. But the words were unfamiliar, sung by a chorus and flowing out of the speakers of the portable tape recorder.

There's a valley in Spain called
  Jarama
It's a place that we all know so well
It was there that we fought the fas-
  cists
We saw a peaceful valley go to
  hell . . .

It didn't quite scan, and Lindsey had
heard better singing. But he listened to a
couple more verses, until the singers put a
lock on it:

We were men of the Lincoln Bri-
  gade
We were proud of the fight that we
  made
We know that you people of the
  valley
Will remember the Lincoln Brigade.

The tape player belonged to an artist
sitting nearby at an easel. He was just
finishing a portrait of an overweight
blonde in a bulging tank top. The woman
accepted her picture and handed some
bills to the artist, looking pleased. There

was a trick to making that much flesh look voluptuous rather than flabby, and this artist had done it.

The woman headed for a shady restaurant a few yards away. Lindsey turned his attention to the artist. The man had dispensed with his beret and wore a straw hat instead. He was clean-shaven and he was old, but his hands and arms looked strong.

'Mr. Bruninski.' Lindsey hoped the man wouldn't bolt. 'Please listen to me. You have to listen to me. You have to tell me, is your wife still alive?'

The man looked up at Lindsey from his wooden folding chair. 'What are you talking about?' He spoke in a strong, harsh voice, studying Lindsey's face all the while. 'What did you call me?'

'Benjamin Bruninski. Israel and Vera's son.' Lindsey consulted his notebook. 'Born February 5, 1916.'

'Don't remind me,' the old man said. 'That was a long time ago. Sometimes I see people half my age go by this corner, and I think, I'm just like them, I have a lot of years ahead of me. Then I remember. If I forget, my knees remind me. I'm an old man, Mister — '

'Lindsey. Hobart Lindsey. I've been looking for you, Mr. Bruninski.'

Bruninski started to get up. Lindsey could see he was stiff with his years. He offered a hand. The old man ignored it. Once he reached his feet the old man stood six inches taller than Lindsey.

'What do you want?'

'Is Mae still alive?' Lindsey asked.

The old man did not answer.

'If she's still alive, she's in terrible danger. There's a man named Nathan ben Zinowicz. He's in New Orleans, and he wants to kill her, and he knows where you live. He stole your file from Peabody's and he wants to kill your wife.'

The old man looked concerned now, no longer merely puzzled. 'You'd better explain this to me.'

Lindsey didn't have time to tell the whole story. 'Your wife is named in a life insurance policy. She stands to collect a fortune, but this man ben Zinowicz wants to stop her, and we have to get the police to stop him. We — '

'Can you prove any of this?'

Lindsey fished a business card from his pocket and handed it to the old man. Bruninski studied the card, stared at Lindsey with overt skepticism, then seemed to make a decision. He barked, 'No police,' making a slashing gesture with one hand.

'Mr. Bruninski — this man is a killer.'

'No police. I'll handle this.' He folded his easel and chair and carried them and his sketching paper and supplies and boom box to the corner restaurant. He must have been friends with the staff. A young woman put down her tray and took Bruninski's belongings into a back room.

Bruninski set off in front of the St. Louis Cathedral and the Cabildo, across St. Ann Street, plowing through clusters of tourists, Lindsey in his wake.

'This man of yours is after Mae, is he? Has my address? He's in for a little surprise, I think.' Bruninski kept walking. Despite his stiffness, his legs were longer than Lindsey's and he was in good shape. Lindsey had to fall into a dogtrot to keep up with the old man.

'What can you do?' Lindsey panted. 'He may be armed. He's capable of anything! Years ago, he shot me in the foot. It still gets sore. Let's stop a police officer and get help.'

Bruninski made his cutting gesture again. 'No police.' They passed St. Philip, Ursulines. They were nearing the edge of the Quarter. Bruninski turned away from the river and kept striding.

The sun had sunk in the river now, and the city was transforming itself. Music and revelry filled the street. Mule-drawn carriages passed, full of tourists, the drivers calling out the historic sites of the Quarter.

The house was on Barracks at Dauphine. It looked as if it had seen better days. The faded, uneven stucco had been whitewashed many times and the wooden shutters had long since lost their paint.

Bruninski stopped and looked up. Lindsey followed his lead. The second-story apartment had a small wrought-iron balcony that held rows of flower pots and planters. The windows were shut and covered with thin, yellowish curtains that

265

were illuminated by light from inside the room.

Bruninski exclaimed, 'My God! The lights are on!'

'But it's night.'

'You'll see.' Bruninski put his hands on Lindsey's shoulders. Lindsey felt as if the old man could throw him across Barracks Street.

'You get out of here if you want to be safe,' Bruninski husked at Lindsey. 'If you come with me, you have to stay behind me and you have to play it by ear. It's up to you.'

Bruninski started up the four cement steps that led to the front door, his sore knees evidently bothering him. The door was unlocked. Bruninski looked around the building's tiny front hall. There was no one there. He took a deep breath, grasped the iron banister with one hand, and began working his way up the stairs. At the upper landing he stopped and pressed his ear against the door, then reached into a pocket of his old khaki pants and silently withdrew a key. He fitted it into the lock and swung the door open.

Lindsey stood on the landing behind Bruninski. He heard a shout of rage and saw the old man launch himself. It was an amazing move. His joints might be stiff, but Bruninski had the muscles of an athlete. He seemed to fly across the room. Lindsey took two rapid steps and was across the threshold.

Even after his years in prison, there was no mistaking Nathan ben Zinowicz. He leaned over the bed, a pillow in his hands. A heavy rectangle of wood lay nearby, and the side of ben Zinowicz's face nearer to Lindsey's view was reddened and abraded as if he had been struck by the wooden beam. An old woman lay on the old bed, staring with terrified eyes at the three men. Lindsey made a mental photograph in a single, frozen instant, then the players snapped into action.

Bruninski crashed into ben Zinowicz. The pillow flew from ben Zinowicz's hands. Bruninski was moving like an aged demon. The two men crashed into a window. The sounds of panes smashing cut through the thud of bodies and the gasping of breath.

Lindsey crossed the room in three more strides. Ben Zinowicz had squirmed out of Bruninski's grip and crouched, facing the older man. Still half-erect, he fumbled to pull a revolver from his trousers pocket. Lindsey made a grab for ben Zinowicz's gun-hand, grasping the wrist in both of his hands. Ben Zinowicz was cursing steadily. He pounded his free hand into the side of Lindsey's head once, twice.

Bruninski had pulled himself painfully to his feet. Ben Zinowicz occupied Lindsey's attention, but somehow Lindsey became aware that Bruninski had reappeared. He saw the old man swing something dark and deadly-looking. It caught ben Zinowicz across the temple.

Ben Zinowicz's fingers closed and a shot crashed harmlessly into the ceiling. The gun tumbled from his hand and ben Zinowicz stumbled across the beam that lay crookedly near a tattered armchair, falling to the bare hardwood floor.

Bruninski stood over them, a huge black revolver in his hand. It looked three times the size of the one ben Zinowicz had dropped. 'I brought this back from Spain,' he panted.

Lindsey lifted the weapon that ben Zinowicz had dropped. He stared at it briefly, found what he hoped must be the safety, and put the revolver in his own pants pocket.

Bruninski was at the bedside, leaning solicitously over the woman who lay in unmoving silence. She was old and obviously very ill. Her wispy gray hair was disordered; her face drawn. Lindsey wondered if she could move or speak.

But her eyes had not changed. They were the green eyes of *La Pasionaria*. They were the green eyes of the woman on the cover of *I Was a Lincoln Brigadier*, of the buxom wench on the cover of *Buccaneer Blades*, of the gun moll on the cover of *Al Capone's Heirs*.

They were the eyes of the woman on the cover of *Death in the Ditch*.

17

She was alive; and her husband, Benjamin Bruninski, tended to all her needs.

Ben Zinowicz was moaning and stirring while Lindsey secured his hands behind him and his ankles to each other, accomplishing the task with his own belt and Benjamin Bruninski's.

There was no telephone in the apartment, so Lindsey pounded down the stairs and across Barracks Street to a nearby saloon and used the pay phone there to call the police. They arrived soon after he got back to the apartment.

They took a quick report from Bruninski and another from Lindsey, who was happy to give them the revolver he'd taken from ben Zinowicz. Bruninski's heavier weapon had disappeared while Lindsey was making his telephone call.

A woman officer called in an inquiry, listened, nodded, and shut off her belt radio. Another officer was present, but the woman seemed to be in charge.

She had already examined Lindsey's ID. The police had removed the belts that Lindsey used to secure ben Zinowicz, but they insisted on keeping them, presumably as possible evidence.

The gray-bearded ben Zinowicz was sitting on the floor now, his hands cuffed behind his back. The heavyset officer asked, 'Are you Nathan ben Zinowicz, sir?'

'I want my rights.'

'There's a fugitive warrant out for Nathan ben Zinowicz. He violated parole in the State of California. If you are Mr. ben Zinowicz — '

'I'm a doctor of philosophy. I want my rights.'

The officer pulled a card from her pocket and read the familiar Miranda warning. When she finished she asked, 'Do you understand that, sir?'

'Damned right I do, and I want a lawyer. Stop asking me questions. Get me a lawyer, or give me a telephone and I'll get my own.'

The heavyset woman sighed. 'All right,

sir. You'll have to come with us, and you can contact a lawyer from the station.' To the other police officer she said, 'We'll put him in the car in a minute. I have to talk to these other people.' She bent over the bed and asked Mae Bruninski a question.

Benjamin Bruninski said, 'She can't talk. She had a stroke. Can't . . . ' His voice trembled.

The police officer said, 'Sir, I think this woman belongs in the hospital. I can call for an ambulance.'

'We've been together since 1937. Through thick and thin. Since 1937.'

Lindsey stared at the old man. Earlier, he had looked younger than his eighty years. Suddenly, he looked older.

'We don't have any money,' Bruninski told the officer. 'The landlord lets us pay what we can. When we can. I make a little money doing sketches. We can't afford a hospital.'

Lindsey said, 'Yes, you can, Mr. Bruninski. Don't you understand? I explained this to you. Mrs. Bruninski has $3,000,000 coming to her. She's — you're millionaires. She was the model for

Death in the Ditch, wasn't she?'

Bruninski nodded.

'She's Alfred Crocker Vansittart's beneficiary. She can afford care.'

Bruninski turned tear-filled eyes on Lindsey. 'This is her home. She'll die in the hospital. I know it. She used to be a nurse — that was how we met. She nursed me and Alfred both, in Spain. She knows what happens to people in hospitals.'

Bruninski blinked, then went on. 'Her name was Maizie Carcowitz then. She changed it when she started to model in Chicago, years later. Alfred and I were both in love with her and she picked me, goddamn it. And I won't send her to a hospital to die!'

To the senior police officer, Lindsey said, 'He may be right. Could you get a doctor to come out here? Make a house call?'

'I guess I could. I'll call it in and see.' To her associate she said, 'Okay, let's get this gentleman out of here. He'll have some local charges to deal with. Then we'll see what happens about returning

273

him to California.' To Lindsey she said, 'I hope you'll be in town a little longer. We'll need your help, sir.'

'I'm at the Monteleone. I'll call you before I do anything like leaving.'

He got another New Orleans Police Department card to add to his growing collection.

Maizie Carcowitz Bruninski, the breathtaking model Mae Carter, moved her hand feebly in Lindsey's direction.

Bruninski said, 'Her mind is clear. We have ways of communicating. She can hold a pencil and write a little, and we have other ways. She wants you to come over by her.'

Lindsey leaned over the old woman. The pillow was back beneath her head — at least the cops hadn't seized that as evidence. Her gray hair was spread around her face. She lifted her hand and touched the back of Lindsey's. Her fingers on the back of his hand felt like the touch of a spider. He looked into her face and detected the shadow of a smile. The eyes were the eyes of *La Pasionaria*.

The doctor came to Barracks Street

and checked Mae Bruninski. He chatted briefly with the two police officers. Nathan ben Zinowicz still sat on the floor, a yard from the beam that had earlier crashed into his head. Soon the police departed, taking ben Zinowicz with them.

The doctor stayed behind. He had a lot to say, mostly about residential care, but the gist of it was that she was stable and could live on as she was, with nourishment and attention. Eventually, nature would take its course. Maybe tomorrow, maybe in ten years. Then he departed, leaving behind a stack of prescription slips.

Bruninski brought a glass of tea to his wife's bedside and held it while she drank a little. Then he turned away. 'She's sleeping,' he said. 'Sit down. She doesn't get enough company. If she wakes up and she hears us talking, she'll like it. Sit. Talk.'

Lindsey lowered himself into a wooden chair. He asked, 'Who hit him with that wooden beam?'

The old man grinned wolfishly. 'Look

over the door there. My little booby trap. You open the door a crack, reach in and disarm the trigger, nothing's gonna happen. When you go out, you re-arm it. Somebody comes in, doesn't know about booby traps, gets conked. Mae can't protect herself these days, and I can't stay with her all day; I have to work. So we set Comrade Wood up there. First time that thing ever had to do its job. Really should have put that skunk out of action. Looks like it just slowed him down. But that was enough, thank God.' He dropped into an armchair. 'You talk, I'll listen. I didn't know Vansittart was dead. And what's this about $3,000,000?'

'It was all over the TV.'

Bruninski gestured. 'No TV.'

Lindsey told him the story, starting with the helicopter crash at Lake Tahoe. By the time he came to Buddy Peabody's story of the missing file, Bruninski said, 'All right. Break time.'

He shuffled to the bathroom. When he came out he walked to his wife's bedside, leaned over her, touched her gently, then turned back. He crossed to a cupboard, opened it, and lifted out a bottle of wine and two mismatched glasses. He poured a glass of wine for himself and one for Lindsey without asking, then handed a glass to Lindsey and touched his own to its rim. '*Salud y suerte.*' He emptied half his glass, then refilled it. 'So she gets . . . how much?'

Lindsey explained the proviso in Vansittart's policy that provided International Surety with a 25% finder's fee if they were able to pay the money to Mae.

'I see.' Bruninski grinned wolfishly. 'So you're acting out of conscience and good will. And to save your company a million bucks.'

'I can't deny it. But you still get a fortune. Your wife does.' He leaned forward. 'Do you have any idea why Vansittart would specify his beneficiary that way? As 'the woman on the cover' instead of by name? Did you ever know Vansittart? Did Mae?'

'Sure, I knew him. We were together in Spain. We were together in the Brigade.'

'He was a communist?'

'No, no.' Bruninski shook his head and

sipped his wine more slowly. 'There were a lot of communists in the brigade, sure, but a lot of us weren't. We were just fighting fascism over there.'

'Even so.' Lindsey got up and walked to the front window. 'I'd have thought — nobody ever knew, did they?'

'Half the guys in the brigade took false names. We were as different as we could be, Albert and I. He was a blue-blood, an old American, filthy rich. My parents came from Poland; we were dirt-poor Jews. But Albert saw something in Franco and in his pals Hitler and Mussolini that most members of his class couldn't see. That's why he volunteered. But he knew he'd have to go home sooner or later, so he gave out the story that he was on an extended European vacation. He was in my company. We were both wounded at Belchite. We both fell in love with a nurse.'

The old man emptied the last of the wine bottle into his own glass. 'After the war the three of us wound up in Chicago. We were all young and crazy. Maizie called herself Mae Carter. Albert and I both wanted to marry her. She picked me. Isn't that rich? But he never stopped carrying the torch for her, did he? That's why he never married.' He jerked his head up. 'You saw my painting at Peabody's gallery, did you?'

Lindsey nodded. 'You still want it back?'

'It's the best thing I ever did. Sure I want it back — for me. I want to look at it. I want *her* to look at it.' He nodded toward the bed. 'After we're both dead, it can go to a museum. If anybody has the brains to see how good it is.'

'I'm sure they will.'

'I'll cut a deal with that s.o.b. Peabody. Five hundred dollars he pays me, and he tries to sell it for $50,000. I'll get it back.' He went to the cupboard and returned with another bottle of wine, then refilled both their glasses. 'You're not drinking much.'

Lindsey shook his head. 'I just don't drink very much, that's all.'

'I kept a few copies of *I Was a Lincoln Brigadier*,' Bruninski said. 'I keep thinking maybe somebody will reprint it someday. Dumb, eh?'

'Not dumb. I think people should know. Somebody has to care. Historians, universities.'

'When I think of the boys who are still there . . . ' Bruninski sighed. 'Girls, too. There were all those nurses. And we had a few girls in the fighting units, too. Nobody knows exactly how many. A lot of records; they wound up in Russia. Thank God they're starting to come out now. There must have been 40,000 volunteers in Spain, maybe 3,000 Americans and boys and girls from countries all over the world. Thousands died. Half of the Americans, at least. Untrained, lousy equipment, garbage for food. But still we could have won, you know. We were in the right, we had passion, we cared. And we were learning how to fight.'

He lowered his glass. Lindsey could see that his eyes were trained on a distant land and a long-ago war.

'But the embargo, you know?' he growled. 'Can you fight a tank with a rifle? Can you shoot down a Stuka with a revolver? I put that in my painting, but that was symbolic, yes? That was my darling Mae, shooting down that fascist plane with a revolver. If we'd just had the equipment, we could have won that war. History would have been different.'

'What happened after you came home?' Lindsey asked.

'Juan Negrin took a chance and sent us all back. The Loyalists still held Madrid. Negrin thought he could get Hitler and Mussolini to pull their forces out, let the Spanish people settle their own differences. The Republic would have won. But they didn't pull 'em out. So the Spanish got Franco and the world got a great big war.'

'But after you came home . . .'

'That was in '38. Henry Ford gave me a ticket back on the *He de Paris*. You didn't know that he paid the freight for us to come home, did you? Fascist anti-Semite that he was. Go figure. I went over on the *Ile de France* and came home on the *Ile de Paris*. Some class, hey?'

'And then what?' Lindsey asked. 'You were only twenty-two years old. What happened then? And why does Rabbi

Bruninski's book say that you died in Spain?'

'The first thing they did was take away our passports. *Not valid for travel to Spain*, right? And we'd fought in a foreign war, we'd violated the Neutrality Act, so I guess we were some kind of criminals. Dangerous men. We'd gone and fought for democracy while Roosevelt sat in the White House reading murder mysteries, feeding morsels to little Fala, and playing footsie with the pope.'

'When was that? When did you actually get back from Spain?'

'The farewell parade in Barcelona was October '38. Cheering crowds, big speeches. You must have heard of *La Pasionaria*. The real one, not the painting. I used Mae in that painting in her honor. We thought we'd won. We thought Franco would fold up. Hitler and Mussolini would pull out and the Republic would live. Hah! Were we ever wrong.'

He downed a slug of wine. 'I got home in time for Christmas. We had a few stragglers, but everybody was out by early

'39. FDR was still playing both sides against the middle. Chamberlain and Daladier and the rest of them.'

'Wasn't that the time of the Hitler-Stalin Pact?'

Bruninski shook his head. 'Nah. That came a little later. Stalin wanted to cut a deal with France, England, America. Nobody would touch him. He remembered what happened during the Revolution, the Russian Civil War, the interventions. Bet they don't teach you about that, about Czechs and Japanese and God knows who else tramping around Russia trying to stop Lenin and put the Whites back in the saddle. And the Americans. That wonderful idealist Woodrow Wilson, who kept us out of war until he got us into it, sent his uniformed thugs in, too.'

'I didn't know that.'

'Look it up. Read the real histories.' He took a drink and resumed his story. 'They took away my passport right on the dock, and I got on the subway and went home to Brooklyn. My mother was surprised to see me. I'd fed her that cock-and-bull story about working in a factory, but she knew the truth, and she thought I was dead. She was amazed; hysterical. She thought I was a ghost.'

'Yes, you must have been reported dead. But where was Mae during all this?'

'Oh, she came down with dysentery and influenza and a couple of other diseases. You have to understand, conditions were pretty primitive up on the lines. A lot of the nurses got sick. They shipped them off to France or to England. By the time Mae got back to the US, we were in the war, and I was in the army. Mae found my mom and got my address and she wrote to me, but she was in service too. We didn't get together again until the war was over.'

'You told me you all went to Chicago.'

'We did, after the Second World War. I was an art student . . . I drew cartoons for the brigade paper over in Spain. And Mae was working again. We got married.'

'You went to work for Paige then, right?'

'Yes. I went to work for Werner Kleinhoffer. He was an idealist. He'd seen what fascism was all about. He was in the

International Brigades too. He was a Bog Soldier. An anti-Hitler German. They weren't all Nazis. Not the Bog Soldiers. Not the boys in the Thaelmann Brigade. We used to drink together when we got a couple of days' leave in the cities. Erich Weinert, Ernst Busch. Good boys. I met Werner for the first time in a whorehouse in Barcelona. Ran across him again a dozen years later in Chicago.'

He leaned toward Lindsey, pointing a long, roughened finger. 'You think I wrote that book, don't you? *I Was a Lincoln Brigadier*. I only wrote part of it. The part in America. The part in Spain, Werner wrote as much of that as I did.'

He leaned away from Lindsey and struggled to his feet. 'Bloody sore knees. Arthritis. Got it in those damned ice-cold foxholes in the Battle of the Bulge.'

'Then you fought Hitler in Europe.'

Bruninski grinned. 'They didn't know what to do with us at the start of the war. They had a name for us. *Premature antifascists*. Stuck us in something called Branch Immaterial. You won't find anything about that in your goddamn military histories of the glorious war. Criminals, homosexuals and premature antifascists.'

Lindsey looked out the window. It was nearly dawn. He'd have to speak with Aurora Delano in a few hours and have her take charge of Bruninski and his wife. International Surety had an obligation to fulfill.

'After the war, Mae and I were married. We decided to stay in Chicago.'

'Why did Paige Publications go out of business, and why did you disappear when you did?' Lindsey asked.

'Because we were premature antifascists, that's why. Then when Uncle Sam finally got around to mixing it up with Hitler and Mussolini, he didn't know what to do with us. The longer the war went on, Uncle Sam was getting close to the bottom of the barrel, so we were rehabilitated and sent to fight.

'After the war there was a little honeymoon; everybody loved everybody. Then Truman decided that socialism was spreading too fast in Europe, and besides, the war industries had wound down in the US and he was afraid of another depression, so he started up the cold war.

'He was taking a lot of heat from the politicians, too,' Bruninski continued. 'HUAC was riding high — Martin Dies and what's-his-name, that thug from New Jersey, Congressman J. Parnell Thomas. Son of a bitch wound up in jail. And of course anybody that HUAC missed, Senator Joe McCarthy took care of. Tailgunner Joe from the great state of Wisconsin, one of America's premier scoundrels.'

He grunted and drank his wine. 'Yes, they sent snoops and spooks and goons around to see us. They shut Paige Publications down. They'd go and see people, ask questions here, plant fear there. A couple of them came around to my studio one day. I was out delivering a job and Mae was in the studio cleaning up. They scared the daylights out of her.' Bruninski bared his teeth. 'I walked in and they were asking her questions, wanting to know if we were getting money from the Politburo, were we members of the CPUSA, what was her opinion of Josef Stalin, where was your husband, was he at a cell meeting, and did she realize that people were spying on their own country and committing treason, and could she give them the name of the person who issued her husband's orders — '

He stood up and checked on his wife's condition. Then he went and stood with his back to the window. 'I grabbed those sons of bitches and I told them if they didn't get out of there and leave us alone I'd bang their heads together until their brains were scrambled.' He showed his teeth again.

'You want to know who those two goons were, Lindsey? They were young Roy Cohn and young Bobby Kennedy. There's your sainted Kennedy clan in action. The old man practically wanted to kiss Hitler's ass when he wasn't busy kissing the pope's ring. And young Bobby got his start working for Tailgunner Joe McCarthy.'

Lindsey stood up. 'Look, I have to go. I'll have our local office contact you today.'

'Tell you what, you walk around the block while I take care of Mae. She needs her breakfast, and I'll clean her up. Come back in half an hour.'

Lindsey agreed. He left the apartment and strolled down toward the river. When he got back, he saw that Mae was propped up in bed. Her hair was brushed and she wore a fresh nightgown. A bedside radio was murmuring. Something that might have been a smile flickered across Mae's face. Lindsey said, 'Hello, Mrs. Bruninski. It's nice to see you this morning.' Then he helped Bruninski lift the wooden beam back into place. Bruninski re-armed the booby trap and they left. They walked to the Café du Monde and ordered coffee with chicory and a platter of *beignets*.

Lindsey's curiosity had been piqued by Bruninski's passionate story. He asked, 'What happened after you threw Roy Cohn and Bobby Kennedy out?'

'They were vindictive sons of bitches. They shut down Paige for publishing those books and for not turning me in. And they didn't like dealing with an old

Bog Soldier, either. Not with the German Democratic Republic starting to get on its feet.' He swallowed half a *beignet* and washed it down with coffee. 'You pay for the refills?'

Lindsey grinned. 'Sure.'

'Werner could have turned his coat and gone to Washington and cried and repented like some of them did. Hell, they had him by the short hairs. But Werner never flinched, even when they put him out of business. They didn't come by and padlock the place; they just saw to it that nobody would distribute his stuff. He got the message pretty quick. Not quick enough for old Izzy Horvitz, though.'

'You knew Horvitz? Del Marston?'

'We were in Spain together. He was clever, a sweet guy. Wrote poetry. He was going to write great novels someday. We got back to the States and wound up in Chicago. Hell, I was the one who got his book published.'

'How did you do that?'

'Izzy wanted to write serious literature, but he wanted to cut his teeth on some kind of popular stuff first. So he wrote this goofy gangster novel. He said it was a hardboiled, whatever that is. He gave it to me to read but I just gave it to Werner. I left it on his desk with a note on it that said, 'Here, this might make a good book for the company.'

'So the next thing I knew,' Bruninski continued, 'Izzy called me up. He's all excited. He sold his book. Werner bought it, he tells me. Then Werner sends the manuscript back to me and he says, 'Okay, now paint a cover for this thing.' And he jots down a few notes about what he wants me to put in the painting. We used to work that way, to save me reading these books.

'I painted the picture for the book, and Mae posed for it. Izzy was so proud; Werner threw a little party for him. Izzy went around autographing everybody's copy of the book. I think I still have mine someplace. But anyway, there we were at the party. And Werner throws one arm around me and one arm around Izzy and he says, 'Thanks to you, Ben, for reading that book and telling me how good it was.' And I says, 'I didn't read that book.

I just painted what you told me to paint.'
And then Werner said, 'I never read it
either. I thought you had, that's why I
bought the damned thing. I got my idea
for the cover picture from Izzy. I called
him up and told him we were taking the
book, and he had some ideas for the
cover. I wrote them down and sent you
the note with the manuscript.''

'What about Del Marston?' Lindsey
prompted.

'McCarthy's goons found out who Del
Marston was. Once they got their hooks
into poor Izzy, he couldn't stand it, poor
guy. He was kind of a loner, you know.
Funny, a sweet guy, but he never got
married or anything. Just him and his
mother; she brought him over from
Russia when he was just a baby. She was a
Trotskyite. And they threatened to deport
her back to Russia. That would have been
the end of her. Poor Izzy.'

'He didn't just get dizzy then,' Lindsey
said, 'and fall off the roof?'

Bruninski snorted. 'It was raining that
day. Don't be a fool. He went up on the
roof to jump off, and Werner ran after

him, but he couldn't stop him in time. Werner never got over that. But it wasn't his fault; it was those goons' fault. Poor Izzy.' He rubbed his big hand across his face. 'As for me, I could have done the same. I could have gone to Washington and raised my hand and turned in my comrades and said it was all a horrible mistake, and I would have been all right.' He tightened his lips.

'I wouldn't do it. I said, to hell with 'em. But after that, every place I went, they found out and I couldn't get work. I tried using other names. I tried not signing my work. They always found me. I was dead as far as painting was concerned. So I wound up sitting in Jackson Square drawing pastel portraits of fat tourists from the corn belt. Some fun, hey, kiddo?'

Lindsey saw a different light come into Bruninski's eyes. 'But I always kept my greatest canvas. I always kept *La Pasionaria*. Until I had to sell it to buy medicine for my wife. That son of a bitch Peabody. Five hundred bucks, and he wants to sell it for fifty thousand. And the thing is, it's worth it. I know a masterpiece, even if I painted it myself.'

Lindsey said, 'I'll have my colleague Aurora Delano come by and see you. She'll see about getting those prescriptions filled, and medical treatment for Mrs. Bruninski. I'm really glad I found you both. I mean, there will have to be some paperwork, affidavits and all, but we'll start the wheels turning right away. International Surety is a responsible company. Ms. Delano will come by today. I'll tell her where to find you. You'll take her up to Barracks Street, won't you?'

Bruninski nodded. 'Sure.'

Lindsey dropped some money on the table and walked with Bruninski, waiting while the old man retrieved his art equipment and set up at his favorite station. A few minutes later Bruninski was busily sketching tourists again.

Lindsey walked through the French Quarter until he reached the Monteleone. Back in his room he fired up his palmtop computer and logged onto KlameNet/Plus. He had one heck of a report to modem over to Desmond Richelieu.

He climbed into bed and slept for a few hours. Then he got dressed and walked back to the police station to give his statement on the incident at Barracks Street. He promised the police that he would return, if necessary, to testify at ben Zinowicz's trial.

Next he phoned Aurora Delano, who met him in the Monteleone lounge for a light snack. He told her of the previous night's events and she agreed to handle the Vansittart claim for Mae Bruninski rather than leave it for standard International Surety processing.

A couple of hours later, Lindsey was sitting in the cramped cabin of a 757. His hands were shaking. He had found the woman on the cover of *Death in the Ditch*. Justice would be served, the express desire of the decedent would be carried out, and International Surety would save its cool million bucks, making Hobart Lindsey the hero of the day.

Nathan ben Zinowicz was behind bars once again. What charges the New Orleans police would bring, and what chance there was of getting a conviction with Mae Bruninski almost certainly unable to testify, was a puzzle. But in any case, ben Zinowicz's parole had been revoked by Dave Jones, and if he returned to California he was headed back to San Quentin. Once in, he would likely face a murder charge in the death of John Frederick O'Farrell.

Mother was about to marry Gordon Sloane. Lindsey was close to marrying Marvia Plum.

So why were his hands shaking?

18

Lindsey took a cab home from Oakland International airport and let himself into the house on Laurel Drive. Mother was out, probably spending the night at Gordon Sloane's condo. He showered to rid himself of the staleness of travel, and climbed into bed. Within minutes he was asleep.

He was awakened by the telephone. Blinking, he read the time. It was 5:30 in the morning. He picked the handset up to hear Mrs. Blomquist's familiar voice. 'Stand by for Mr. Richelieu, please.'

'Lindsey,' Richelieu began, 'I just pulled your report off KNP. Are you sure you've found the bennie?'

'I tracked her, Mr. Richelieu. It's all there in my report. Mrs. Bruninski is definitely the woman on the cover of *Death in the Ditch*.'

'Fingerprints? Documentation? Witnesses?'

'Harkins knew both Bruninskis in Chicago. We can get a deposition if we have to. But *La Pasionaria* proves it. That's the same model as the book covers, the Lincoln Brigade book and the other Paige books as well as *Death in the Ditch*. And that's the same woman. I saw her. She isn't in good shape, and the years have changed her, but she is definitely the same woman.' He added, 'She was an army nurse in World War II. There should be fingerprints on file at the Pentagon. Aurora Delano is handling the case in New Orleans, but this woman is for real, count on it.'

Richelieu said, 'For once it's to our advantage to pay the claim, not deny it. I've already talked to Legal. They're rolling. And don't think I don't trust you, Lindsey, but I had a little chat with Aurora Delano this morning.'

'And?'

'Delano speaks well of you, too. What about the painting? You didn't spend my fifty grand, did you?'

'No, sir. I was only after it as a way to reach Bruninski. Once I found him without it, I didn't need the painting anymore. And once ben Zinowicz got the address out of the files at the gallery, nobody really needed it anymore. Besides, Bruninski's going to try and get it back from the gallery for himself and his wife. She was a real beauty, believe me.'

As he spoke, Lindsey heard the front door of the house open and close.

'Not interested,' Richelieu ground out. 'Let Bruninski have it.'

'You mean you want him to buy it back from Peabody for a hundred times what Peabody paid him for it?'

'That's his problem, Lindsey. Here's yours. You'd better go get a sign-off from Mr. and Mrs. Cooke. Do it quickly.'

As Lindsey showered, he resolved to have Aurora Delano help Bruninski get back his painting. Offer Peabody a nice price for the painting, but nothing like fifty grand. And if he refused, threaten him with a high-profile lawsuit. *Greedy art dealer exploits starving genius*. He'd come around.

When Lindsey came out, he found Mother in the kitchen. She turned from the stove and held her face up for a good-morning kiss. Lindsey slid into his chair and buttered a slice of toast for himself.

Sloane had dropped Mother at the house while Lindsey was on the telephone. After breakfast she dressed for her job. Lindsey changed into a fresh suit, dropped Mother at her work, then drove on to the International Surety office on North Broadway.

He telephoned the World Fund for Indigent Artists in San Francisco. A cultured female voice answered. He identified himself and asked to speak with Mr. or Mrs. Cooke. Lindsey was sure the Cookes were behind both the killing of John O'Farrell and the attempt on his own life. And they were more than likely responsible for the death of Albert Crocker Vansittart and the helicopter crash at Lake Tahoe. Cooke claimed to have known Vansittart's son — a son who never existed. The Cookes would have known about the International Surety policy on Vansittart's life — that information would have been in WFIA's files since its early days in Chicago. And they had every reason in the world for trying to thwart Lindsey's search for the prime beneficiary. How would they react to his phone call today?

He was put through. 'Mr. Cooke, I have some very important news for you,' Lindsey said. 'I think we'd better discuss this face to face.'

'All right. My office. One hour.' Cooke rang off.

Lindsey headed downstairs and started for San Francisco. He left his car at the transit station and rode a train through the tube on the bottom of San Francisco Bay. Once he reached his stop and rode the escalator to street level, he walked to 101 California. An hour after leaving home he was in the lush reception area of the World Fund for Indigent Artists.

Cooke kept him waiting for more than an hour. When Lindsey finally faced him in his office, the man was not in a pleasant mood.

'The primary beneficiary of Albert Crocker Vansittart's life policy has been located,' Lindsey told him. 'The World

Fund will receive no payment. Just for the record, International Surety would appreciate your signing an acknowledgment of that and a quit-claim on the matter.'

Cooke sneered at him.

'I have a quit-claim form right here,' Lindsey volunteered. 'I.S. might even offer a modest settlement — I mean, really a very modest settlement — in exchange, just to clear the matter. We don't need your sign-off, you understand,' Lindsey added. 'International Surety is going to pay the beneficiary. You're not going to receive anything in any case.'

'We'll tie you up, Lindsey. You don't have a chance. Tell you what, you pay that money to the World Fund and we'll just drop the matter.'

'Mr. Cooke, I want you to understand that I know all about Nathan ben Zinowicz.'

There was a short silence. Then, 'Is this blackmail?'

'Nothing like. I just wondered, have you heard from him lately?'

'That's none of your business.'

Lindsey smiled. 'Is that so? Well, he's in jail.'

Cooke's eyes widened. 'Where?' he demanded.

Lindsey rose and headed for the exit. He could hardly contain himself. Then he passed Cynthia Cooke, looking suddenly two decades older than she had over lunch at Liberté, scurrying toward her husband's office. Lindsey said, 'Good morning, Mrs. Cooke. Maybe I'd better stay a little longer after all?'

She preceded him into her husband's office, turned back and hissed, 'You wait here.' He stepped backwards barely in time to avoid catching a face full of door.

He rode the elevator down to the lobby, found a pay phone and reached Marvia at Berkeley Police Headquarters. As soon as she recognized his voice she said, 'Hold onto your hat. This thing is getting exciting. Where are you now?' He told her. 'Get out of there. Put some distance between yourself and the Cookes *now*.'

'Why?'

'Please, Bart, just do it. You can call me back later. If I'm not here they'll patch you through to me. Just do it!'

Lindsey hung up and left the building. He walked through the city, winding up in North Beach, at the Washington Square Bar & Grill. There he ordered a glass of mineral water from the bartender, made his way to the pay phone, and dialed Berkeley again. When he reached Marvia he asked, 'What was that all about?'

'Your old friend, Dr. ben Zinowicz, is under arrest in New Orleans.'

'I know that. I was there when they took him away. Are you getting him back? I mean, are they sending him back to California? Does Dave Jones have to go after him, or what?'

'We'll work that out. It won't be easy, but I don't think a man like ben Zinowicz would relish doing time at Angola. He just might prefer to come back to California. Otherwise, it's up to the DAs and the State Attorneys. Bart, I have to talk to you. Right away. Where are you now?' He told her. 'Look, can you wait for me there? I need to talk to you.'

He said okay, and replaced the handset.

Then he went for a short walk about the hilly neighborhood. The sky was gray and the air was chilly and wet. When he got back he stood in front of the entrance, waiting for Marvia. The change in climate from New Orleans was dramatic, but Lindsey was so caught up in the events of recent days that he hardly noticed the cold.

He held out his hands to Marvia as she arrived, and she took his. She was wearing a quilted jacket against the day's chill, and a pair of faded jeans. She looked beautiful.

Together they went back inside the bar and grill. The lunch crowd was thinning now, and they were able to get a table in the main dining room. Lindsey was surprised when Marvia ordered a whiskey, neat. She smiled briefly at his expression. 'I'm off duty. I clocked out after you called the second time.'

The waiter brought Marvia's drink and dropped two menus on the white linen cloth. Marvia picked up her drink and downed half of it. She squeezed her eyes shut and Lindsey thought he could see a

305

flush in her face, despite her very dark coloring. He asked, 'What's wrong?'

'Bart, let's catch up on this Vansittart case. The rest can wait — maybe we'll take a walk afterwards, and talk things over.'

Something cold sent its tendrils through him. All he could think of to say was, 'Okay.'

The waiter returned and took their orders. Neither ordered a heavy meal.

Marvia said, 'Tell me about New Orleans.'

He told her the whole story.

'And Bobby Kennedy and Roy Cohn personally hounded him out of the publishing world, and destroyed his career?'

'That's what he told me.'

'Doesn't sound right to me.' Marvia picked at her crab meat salad. 'I thought they worked for Joe McCarthy.'

'Yes. Bruninski mentioned McCarthy, too. Maybe he got them mixed up. I mean, he's an old man. It's been a long time.'

'Is he a good painter? You told me one

of his pieces was priced at $50,000. That sounds like a pretty good painter to me.'

Lindsey nodded. 'I thought his old book covers were good, competent commercial pieces. Ditto his pastel portraits for tourists in Jackson Square in New Orleans. His customers were happy, anyway.'

'What about the painting?'

'I think it's worth every penny. His wife had a stroke. She's bedridden. He was hounded for years, his career destroyed. They were living from hand to mouth. He kept that canvas for forty years. Finally he had to part with it for medicines. I don't think he had any idea what it was worth.'

'Do you think he'll get it back from Peabody?'

Lindsey shrugged. 'Yes, I think Bruninski will get it. Peabody doesn't want that kind of publicity. He'll probably set it up so he gets some good press out of it. You know, 'Humanitarian art dealer returns painting to penniless genius.' Picture in the paper, interview on TV. We'll see.'

'At least the Bruninskis will have money now,' Marvia said. 'They should be comfortable for the rest of their lives. Maybe he can paint another.'

'Not like *La Pasionaria*, Marvia. Believe me, that painting is one of a kind.'

He watched her toying with salad. She hadn't eaten anything. 'What about this end of things?' he asked.

'That's why I wanted you to get away from the Cookes. That's going to blow wide open. We've got SFPD into the act, the Feds are interested, it's huge. And you get credit. If you hadn't poked into the case, and kept on poking, the whole thing might have gone unnoticed.'

'I don't know about that. I mean, Jamie's video was the first sign we had that anything was the matter.'

'Well — the way you tracked down Ben Bruninski and Mae Carter was fine work. And putting ben Zinowicz away again, that was first class. Maybe they'll throw away the key this time.'

The waiter appeared and asked if they wanted anything else. Lindsey had a cappuccino; Marvia ordered an aperitif. Lindsey was a little surprised; he'd never thought of her as a drinker. 'What's going on with the Cookes?' he asked. 'What are the feds and the local police doing?'

He waited. 'Ben Zinowicz is a fool,' she said at last. She lifted her tiny glass and sipped carefully. 'He had an apartment here in the city, but there was just his clothes and his personal clutter in it.'

'Nothing interesting in his Berkeley apartment either. He never really moved in. He just kept his computer there, and he wiped that clean before he disappeared. Or he tried.'

'Right.' She smiled. 'He wiped it clean, but you have to remember that he was a very compulsive self-documenter.'

'I remember that from our first encounter. And Dave Jones told me that the computer people managed to recover his files.'

'That's right. He kept very careful records on his computer. Our little wizards down at headquarters went over that machine, worked some abracadabra on the hard drive and recovered the data he thought he'd wiped. Shades of Watergate!'

'What did they find?'

'He kept an appointment book, but with detailed annotations. The wizards got most of it back, and there's no doubt that he was thick as thieves with the World Fund people. The fund was legitimate at first, but after Mr. and Mrs. Cooke got control of it, they turned it into their personal cash cow. They made a few little grants here and there. But most of what they collected — and it was *lots* — went into supporting them in their posh lifestyle. That, and lining their nest, and of course back into fundraising efforts for the next round of dollars and condos and limos.'

Lindsey tasted the cappuccino. 'What about the O'Farrell murder?'

'He didn't quite say 'I killed O'Farrell,' but his travel plans were there, and cryptic little notes about 'Docs Hosp/ Truckee' and 'Donner turnoff.' My God, the man was tying a noose around his own neck with every keystroke.'

'And the Cookes?'

'We already had a meeting with the DA's office and the US Attorney. We'll have to sort out the jurisdictional

310

problems, but we had a chat with ben Zinowicz in New Orleans, too, and I think he'll talk about the Cookes to save his own rear end. And he's going to need a lot of saving, so I think he's going to do a lot of talking.'

She finished her aperitif and excused herself to visit the ladies' room. Lindsey watched her progress. There was a slight list to her movement. When she returned he suggested a little fresh air. She agreed.

They left the restaurant and crossed the street to Washington Square Park.

19

They walked slowly past the old San Francisco Firemen's Monument and stopped just across the street from St. Peter and St. Paul's. Lindsey said, 'We could go in right now and ask a priest to marry us.'

Marvia turned to him and put her arms around him. He felt her shaking and saw that she was crying. 'I can't marry you.'

He led her to the edge of the park, crossed Filbert Street with his arm still around her, and pushed into the church. It was deserted at this hour. The late-afternoon sun coming through the radial window filled the vestibule with a rainbow of rich colors. Lindsey led Marvia to a pew and they sat together.

She said, 'I'm moving up to Reno.'

He was stunned.

'I want to see this case through first, and clean up the rest of my work, but then I'm resigning from the force.'

'Why, Marvia?'

'Willie Fergus is eligible for early retirement from the Washoe Sheriff's Department. He'll have both his pensions and he can get a security job at a casino. He's already had some offers; they're always eager to get people with law enforcement experience. He thinks I can get a job, too. We'll have enough to live on.'

'Willie Fergus,' Lindsey whispered. He pulled his fingers free of Marvia's. He hit himself on the forehead with the heel of his hand, feeling like a fool, acting like a fool. 'The night I phoned you from New Orleans. I was at the Monteleone and you were at home and Willie Fergus answered the phone. And I didn't even think about it.'

'I'm so sorry, Bart. I love you. I really do. And you've been so good to me, and so good to Jamie. But when I saw Willie again after all those years, I . . . ' She leaned her head on his shoulder and shuddered.

'I should have known. I mean, I hadn't realized about Germany until he told me.

And now he's back.'

'It wasn't like that in Germany. You know I was involved with James Wilkerson then. Willie Fergus was like an uncle to me. He was older, and he was sympathetic. He helped me in such a terrible time. I didn't know where to turn and he helped me.'

'Were you lovers then? Not that I suppose it matters.'

'It *does* matter, Bart. I never lied to you. You knew there were men before you. Men besides James Wilkerson. But not since we've been together. And in Germany, Willie Fergus was my best friend. But that's *all* he was, he was only my friend.'

Lindsey said again, 'I don't suppose it matters.' He straightened his shoulders and took a deep breath. 'You were so good to me too, Marvia. You brought me to life, you know. Before I found you, I was just a kind of zombie. I got up in the morning and went to work and came home at night and just waited for bedtime because I had nothing to do, I had no one. Only Mother, and she was . . . not really there.' Then he said, 'What about Jamie?'

'He'll stay with my mother. He'll be all right. Hakeem's mother will take the boys after school. His father works and his mother stays home.'

'What about Wilkerson? What does he have to say about this?'

'He has nothing to say about it. We've settled with him and his wonderful new wife. He's happy now; he looks like a shoo-in for the House of Representatives. Imagine, a conservative Republican black Gulf War hero freshman Congressman from Texas. He'll be the whitest black man in Congress. He won't want to stir up trouble again over Jamie. He'll want to keep Jamie and me out of the spotlight.'

Lindsey grunted.

'I'm so sorry,' Marvia said. 'Maybe it is the race thing after all. You're so decent, Bart, and I'm hurting you. I don't want to hurt you but I'm doing it. I know it and I can't help it. Willie just *knows* things. He's lived this the same as I have.' She held her hands in front of her face and ran the fingers of one over the back of the other, as if discovering something she'd never seen before. 'He knows what it is. You can't know. It isn't your fault; you just can't know.'

Lindsey reached for her hands again but she pulled them away. She stood up suddenly and drew a deep, shuddering breath. He stood up with her and they walked to the front door of the church. Lindsey pulled a bill out of his pocket and dropped it in the poor box on his way out.

They stood on the sidewalk facing the park. The church behind them cast a long shadow. The heavy clouds were breaking up and the sky overhead was a dark, dark blue, almost purple.

'What do you want to do now?' Lindsey asked.

'I don't know. Nothing. I feel empty, sick. I'm sorry.' She turned and looked up into his face. 'Did you drive in to the city?'

'No. I took the train in.'

'I'll give you a ride back. I can drop you in Berkeley or I can take you to your car.'

He stood there for a minute. Darkness had arrived with amazing suddenness. The sky above Washington Square Park was black. Beyond North Beach, in San Francisco's financial district, Lindsey could see the Transamerica Pyramid reaching for the sky. It looked like a gigantic rocket ship balanced precariously on its tail, waiting for the countdown to end so it could blast free of its foundation and travel to the distant stars. He found himself wishing he could climb aboard the rocket ship and travel with it far, far into space and never return to earth.

'Bart?'

He walked sadly from the launching pad. 'No,' he said. 'Thank you, no. I'll just take the train.'

When he reached Walnut Creek he called his house, hoping that Mother wouldn't answer the phone. She didn't. He heard his own voice on the answering machine. He hung up the pay phone, climbed in his blue Volvo, and drove home.

He paused in the kitchen but he still had no appetite. He went to his room and found the set of Paige books that he'd received in Chicago, and stood studying the colorful covers, especially the ones featuring the lush young model, Mae Carter.

He picked through his small collection of compact disks and selected one that Marvia had given him. It was Mile Davis playing Gershwin's *Porgy and Bess*. He'd listened to it when Marvia gave it to him, but seldom put it on. The music was simply too sad for him. But tonight he played it. He found himself wondering if Miles Davis had been as sad when he played the Gershwin melodies as he was tonight as he listened to them.

A little later he found himself sitting on the rug, listening to the sad music and crying for the aged, crippled, sick Mae Carter, dying slowly in her bed on Barracks Street in the French Quarter.

He didn't remember getting into bed, but the next thing he knew it was morning and he had a headache and a sour stomach and he felt worse than he'd felt in years. At first he didn't know why. Then he remembered his conversation with Marvia.

He sat on the edge of the bed until he had his bearings, then he took a long shower and shaved and dressed. There was no sign of Mother. He wasn't worried anymore. For breakfast he drank a glass of water. It was all he could face.

Before leaving the house he checked the telephone answering machine. There were two messages. One was from the United States Attorney's office in San Francisco. The other was from Desmond Richelieu in Denver. The messages were the same: return call as soon as possible. The only difference was, the message from the US Attorney was polite.

He returned the Federal call first and was invited to come in for a brief chat about the World Fund for Indigent Artists. He made an appointment later the same morning.

When he called SPUDS/HQ, Desmond Richelieu took the call at once. Richelieu was almost friendly. 'Talked to Aurora again. Got the details from her end. Good work, Lindsey. What do you have on your plate now?'

Lindsey squeezed his eyes shut. 'Nothing major, Mr. Richelieu. Some ongoing cases, nothing very big. But I still have to follow up on the Vansittart.'

'Why? What's left to do? I.S. is paying out the three million, saving the million-dollar finder's fee. Bennie's happy, company's happy. What's left?'

'Well, there's Dr. ben Zinowicz and the O'Farrell killing.'

'That belongs to the cops, Lindsey. Don't forget who you are, who pays your salary. Your job is to do your job, not play Eliot Ness.'

'You're right,' Lindsey conceded.

'Anything else?'

'I have an appointment with the US Attorney in, ah, two hours. I just got the message from them. I called them back a few minutes ago and made the appointment. It's about the WFIA — Mr. and Mrs. Cooke.'

'Right. Well, you do have your duty as a citizen.'

In his mind's eye Lindsey saw Richelieu sitting behind his immaculate desk, gazing adoringly at his autographed portrait of J. Edgar Hoover. He asked, 'Is that all? I'll go talk to the US Attorney and then I'll update the file through KNP. Unless you want to talk to me about it.'

'I want to talk to you about a couple of things. Go have your meeting and call me again.' Richelieu paused. Lindsey knew that pause; it was famous throughout International Surety. 'I'll see you at the conference here in Denver, right?'

'With bells on, sir.'

Like a court jester.

★   ★   ★

At the US Attorney's office in the Federal Building in downtown San Francisco, Lindsey was met by a startlingly young woman who introduced herself as Marge Tillotson. She ushered him into a cramped cubicle. He declined her offer of refreshment.

After a minimal amount of paper-shuffling she said, 'This is about the World Fund for Indigent Artists.' She opened a folder and read, 'The fund was created in Chicago, Illinois on One

October 1951. Officers of incorporation were Walter Paige, Bob Brown, and Mae Carter. Do you know any of these people, Mr. Lindsey? Do you happen to know if they're still alive?'

Lindsey happened to know a lot that Marge Tillotson was eager to find out. She jotted notes.

'In 1954,' she continued after a moment, 'the Chicago Artists and Models Mutual Aid Society moved to Washington, D.C., and was renamed the National Welfare League for Graphic Creators. Information on them is not very complete, Mr. Lindsey. The only name we've been able to turn up, connected with this period in the organization's history, is an unincorporated partnership called Kennedy and Cohn. Records are almost nonexistent. Would you happen to know anything about this? Could this possibly be the famous Kennedy family? And could Cohn be the Roy Cohn who was on Senator Joseph R. McCarthy's staff at one time? Have your investigations turned up any information in this regard?'

Lindsey smiled slightly. 'No, I'm afraid not.'

'Why are you smiling?'

'I've come across those names in another context. But nothing to do with what you quoted.'

Tillotson turned a sheet in the manila folder and nodded to herself. 'Early in 1968, Kennedy and Cohn apparently severed their relationship with the N.W.L.G.C. and the organization was taken over by Roger St. John Cooke and Cynthia Cooke. They moved the organization's headquarters to San Francisco, renamed it the World Fund for Indigent Artists, and have run it ever since.' She leaned back in her seat, smiled warmly at Lindsey, and asked, 'What can you add to my knowledge?'

Lindsey responded, 'Is that all you have?'

'Oh, no,' Tillotson replied. She pulled open a desk drawer, removed a small computer, and placed it on her desk. She tapped a few keys and the folding monitor screen came to life. 'Can you see that all right?'

'I can.'

'We have some conflicting laws, Mr. Lindsey.' She touched the computer. 'Income tax returns of course are confidential, and census data, and a lot of other things. The government certainly recognizes the citizens' right of privacy.' Another smile. The smile of the wolf, Lindsey thought. 'On the other hand, the government is supposed to operate in the open. We can't spy on our own citizens. And matters of public record have to be open to the public, don't you see?'

'I've used the Freedom of Information Act a couple of times,' Lindsey told her.

'You see the dilemma we face, though. I can't show you the information I've got on the World Fund and on Mr. and Mrs. Cooke. I can only look it up for my own use, as part of my job. You understand?'

'Sure.'

She tapped a few more keys on the computer and columns of figures scrolled across the screen. 'This isn't happening and you mustn't peep over my shoulder when I consult a confidential file.'

The Cookes drew salaries of a dollar a

year apiece. But they had unlimited expense accounts, and they lived high. In addition to their Nob Hill condo, they owned another in Maui, another in Vail, and another in St. Maarten, as well as six automobiles, a variety of valuable paintings and sculptures with which their homes were decorated, and a gilt-edged stock portfolio. Their wardrobes were not mentioned, but Cynthia Cooke's jewels were.

'I thought they were old money,' Lindsey said. 'Maybe those belongings all came from their inheritances.'

Tillotson grinned. 'No way. We've been tracking the bills and the payments. They did a pretty good job of covering their tracks, but not good enough. World Fund is tax-exempt. That requires pretty stringent financial reporting. We've got 'em six ways to Sunday, Mr. Lindsey.'

'Then why do you need me?'

'Because of the insurance scam they were trying to pull. We haven't figured out completely how it fits in, but we have a pretty good idea.'

'And what's that?'

'The World Fund is not in good shape, Mr. Lindsey. They rent fancy office suites; they furnish them like billion dollar corporate headquarters, staff them with fashion plates . . . well, you've been there, you know the drill.'

'And this makes people give them money?'

'Isn't that something? Like goes to like. Money goes to money. They don't look for nickel-and-dime donations from poor working stiffs. They look for major bequests, endowments, foundation grants. Why struggle for $100,000 worth of five- and ten- and twenty-dollar donations while you ride around in a rusty old Plymouth, live in the Outer Mission, eat at McDonald's? Why not go for a $100,000 grant, ride in a Mercedes, live on Nob Hill, take your meals at Liberté?'

'All on one dollar a year?'

'All on one dollar a year plus expenses. The World Fund pays for everything. Mr. and Mrs. Cooke are going to take a fall, if only for income tax evasion. We put Leona Helmsley away; we're going to get

Roger St. John Cooke and Cynthia Cooke. But there's more to this than tax evasion. What can you tell me about the Vansittart insurance policy?'

Lindsey did a quick internal review of International Surety procedures. There was nothing secret about Albert Crocker Vansittart's odd policy. It had been all over the media since Vansittart's death. And Marge Tillotson would soon be getting the complete lowdown on Nathan ben Zinowicz if she didn't already have it. So he gave her everything.

When he finished his story she picked up her telephone and speed-dialed the County DA's office. Five minutes later she placed the handset back on its cradle and gave Lindsey a long, calculating look. 'I'm always the last to know,' she complained.

'What happened?'

'The local folks have been talking to the authorities in New Orleans. Dr. ben Zinowicz is caught between a rock and hard place. He doesn't want to come back to California and face murder charges in the death of John O'Farrell, and he doesn't want to serve the rest of his old sentence. He's pretty upset with David Jones for revoking his parole, but that's a *fait accompli* now. But he mostly doesn't want to face attempted murder charges in Louisiana and maybe wind up doing long, hard time at Angola.'

Lindsey grinned. This was what he'd hoped for. 'So what happens now?'

'So he wants to cut a deal. He wants Louisiana to let him go. And their case is pretty weak, you know. Then he wants to testify against the Cookes. He knows the insides and the outsides of the World Fund, he can ice the case for us. In return, he wants Louisiana to drop everything, he wants no Federal charges over World Fund, and he wants to cop a plea on O'Farrell.'

Lindsey let out a deep breath. 'Are you going to go for that?'

'I don't have anything to do with the Louisiana charges, but I think they'll be just as happy to have him out of their hair and back in California's. I don't have anything to do with the O'Farrell case either; that's up to California.'

'How about Nevada?'

'I think they're out of it. They could have arm-wrestled California for the privilege of prosecuting O'Farrell for the Vansittart killing, but they're not interested in O'Farrell's death. That's strictly California.'

Lindsey grunted. 'What about the Cookes? I mean, regarding both the Vansittart and O'Farrell killings?'

'Those are up to California. That's where ben Zinowicz comes in with his little vocal performance. I'll bet you a good lunch that ben Zinowicz testifies that the Cookes hired O'Farrell to kill Vansittart, and that they fed ben Zinowicz a mysterious potion with the power to bend his will to theirs, and made him kill O'Farrell.'

This time Lindsey snorted. 'You'll go for that? Madam, I have a wonderful bridge you would love to buy.'

Tillotson leaned across her desk, locking onto Lindsey's eyes with her own. 'Of course I don't buy that, and I'm sure the DA in Washoe County or Placer County or San Francisco — whoever catches the case — won't buy it either. I'm just telling you what I expect to hear.'

Lindsey stood up. 'Can I go now? Do you need me for anything else?'

'I might need you later on, to give me a statement and maybe to talk to a grand jury.'

'Be happy to.'

★ ★ ★

Lindsey got out of San Francisco. As long as he was talking with Marge Tillotson, and as long as he could concentrate on the topic at hand, he didn't have to think about Marvia. But once he was back in his car, headed for the Bay Bridge, it hit him again. There was an aching wound inside him.

He pulled his car into the garage on North Broadway and took the elevator up to the International Surety office. Kari Fielding was in the inner office with Elmer Mueller, and Lindsey found his desk and logged on to KlameNet/Plus. He pulled up the Vansittart file to check on actions since he'd left New Orleans.

Aurora Delano was handling things perfectly. She'd got a quick cash advance for Mae Bruninski, and the paperwork for the full $3,000,000 was moving as fast as it ever did. She'd even had a friendly chat with Buddy Peabody, and it looked as if he was willing to settle up with Bruninski for a small profit and a big publicity break.

Lindsey called Dave Jones in Oakland and learned that ben Zinowicz was on his way back to California in the company of a US marshal. He'd waived extradition and was eager to cut a deal.

Then he called Desmond Richelieu but got only as far as his secretary, Mrs. Blomquist. The director was in a meeting, but Mr. Lindsey was advised to pick up his messages on KNP. There was full data there on the SPUDS conference in Denver.

Lindsey logged onto KNP and downloaded the SPUDS conference schedule. It was time to call the travel agent and make his flight arrangements.

20

Lindsey flew to Denver early Monday morning. As he left Oakland, the sun was a brilliant disk rising over the snow-capped Sierras; the day looked like a beauty.

But Mother's wedding took place the day before Lindsey flew to Denver. And on the morning of the day before the wedding, Lindsey carefully gift-wrapped his set of Paige Publications books and drove to Scotty Anderson's home in Castro Valley. When Anderson admitted him to the apartment, Lindsey ceremoniously extended the brightly wrapped parcel.

Anderson looked suspiciously at the package. 'What's that?'

'A present. Don't you remember me? You helped me out with *Death in the Ditch*. You put me on to Paige Publications. You were working on a bibliography for some fellow named Lovisi.'

'Oh, yeah, sure.' Anderson nodded solemnly. 'Sure, come on in.' Inside the apartment he continued, 'I've kind of stalled on that Paige piece for Lovisi.'

'That's what I've got for you.' Lindsey made a second attempt to hand the parcel to Anderson. This time, the big collector took it.

They had reached Anderson's office. He sat at his desk, waved Lindsey to an easy chair, and carefully opened the parcel, then spread the books across his desk. As he added each one, the expression on his face evolved from pleased, to delighted, to ecstatic.

'Look at that, will you? *Cry Ruffian!*' He moved his hand as if to caress the lurid book, but his fingers did not quite touch the cover. '*Al Capone's Heirs!*' He looked at Lindsey the way the Caliph looked at the evil Jaffar in the Korda *Thief of Bagdad* when he first laid eyes on the flying horse. '*By Studebaker Across America.*' He sighed. 'Do you know what you've brought to me? These are some of the scarcest books in the whole paperback field. These are scarcer than LA Bantams. This is the only *By Studebaker Across America* I've ever seen. It may be the only one in existence.' There were tears in his eyes. 'Where did you get these?'

Lindsey said, 'From Walter Paige's grandchildren. They were saved when the company went under and later when the Paige Building was torn down.'

'And you're giving these to me?' Anderson asked.

'Token of my appreciation.'

'I don't know how to thank you, Mr. Lindsey. I'll make photos of these covers to go with my article for Lovisi's magazine. We'll cop the cover, that's for sure. I know Gary Lovisi's taste, and I'll bet he puts *Teen Gangs of Chicago* on the cover of *Paperback Parade*. This is wonderful, absolutely wonderful.' Then worried look came onto his face. 'Are these a gift? You want to sell them to me, or what?'

'I told you, they're a token of my appreciation. Really. I don't want anything for them. I'm not a collector myself, but I know enough about collectors to understand that things like these books should have a good home. I know you'll give them a good home.'

'That's a promise.'

After leaving Castro Valley, Lindsey drove home to Walnut Creek. Mother was busily packing for her wedding trip. 'You know, your father and I never had a real honeymoon. We thought he'd finish his navy service and I'd finish school and then we could have our honeymoon. And that never happened.'

Lindsey took his mother's hands. 'You're entitled to some happiness. Are you sure you're doing the right thing?'

'Yes, I am.' She freed her hands, opened a closet door and surveyed her shoes. She pulled a pair of leather pumps from the shoe rack and rolled them carefully in an old pillowcase before she put them in her suitcase. 'I've always wanted to see Hawaii. Now I'll have my chance.' Then she turned and looked up into Lindsey's face. 'You know, I have you to thank for this. You and your wonderful Marvia.' She made a funny clicking sound with her tongue. 'You know, at first I almost resented her. Here was this strange woman taking my little boy away from me.' She managed a small smile, then went on. 'I clung to you so; you were all that I had left after your father died. I just couldn't let you grow up. It was bad for you and it was bad for me, I know. I'm sorry, Hobart. I hope you can forgive me.'

'It's all past, Mother.' He hadn't told her about Marvia and Willie Fergus. 'I want you and Gordon to be happy together.' He knew he'd have to tell her sooner or later, but he was content to let it be later. 'You're sure you want to sell the house and move into Gordon's condo?'

Mother actually laughed, a rare event. 'It's too late now. I've already moved half my belongings. Hobart, my little Hobo, I'm going to miss living with you, but I'm grown up now. It's time for me to spread my wings and go out on my own.'

He gave her a hug and looked at his watch. 'What about dinner, Mother? We're due at the Coffmans'.'

'All right. You go away and let me finish this, and then we'll go.'

On the way to the Coffmans' house in Concord, Lindsey clicked a cassette into the Volvo's tape deck. He'd picked up a matched set of oldies compilations, and he put in the tape for 1952, the last full year of his father's life and the year when Lindsey was conceived. It was a big era for vocalists: almost every track featured a solo vocal and an orchestral backing. 'Cry,' sung by Johnny Ray; 'Wheel of Fortune,' by Kay Starr; 'Auf Wiederseh'n, Sweetheart,' by Vera Lynn. The cold war had been hot in 1952, and Germany had been a grim, tense, divided country. How many *fräuleins* had heard that song and wept for their GIs or Tommies or *poilus*? 'You Belong to Me,' by Jo Stafford, and 'I Went to Your Wedding,' by Patti Page.

Mother knew all the words to every song, and she sang along with Johnny and Kay and Vera. Lindsey couldn't remember ever hearing her sing before. She had a pleasant voice. He wondered if she had sung lullabies to him when he was a baby. He couldn't remember. He hoped that she had.

Lindsey laughed when the Patti Page

track came on. Mother asked if the song was that funny, and Lindsey said no, he just happened to know another Patti Paige and the song made him think of her.

'I used to love those songs. We used to sing along with the radio — my girlfriends and I, we used to love the songs.' Mother turned her head toward Lindsey. Her features stood out in the light of oncoming traffic. When Lindsey was growing up she'd always seemed old to him, but now that she was approaching 60, she didn't look old at all. He felt a knot in his chest and silently wished her good health and some good years with her new husband.

They arrived at the Coffmans' house and Miriam greeted them at the door. She embraced Lindsey's mother warmly, then gave Lindsey himself a peck on the cheek and ushered them into the living room. There had to be something between women, Lindsey knew, that would never be revealed to men, or never understood by them even if it could be revealed. Something that was communicated between a married woman and a woman about to be married. What was the message? *Men — what can we do with the big, helpless, sweet things?* Maybe that was the message.

Eric Coffman stood up and embraced Mother and shook Lindsey's hand. Coffman's beard and his waistline were as thick as ever, but the beard was starting to show signs of gray. He led Mother and Lindsey to the couch and offered them a round of drinks; Miriam disappeared from the room and returned, preceded by her daughters. Sarah carried a tray of *hors d'oeuvres*; Rebecca, little plates and napkins. Miriam stood beaming behind the girls as they set their cargo on the table in front of the couch.

Lindsey shot a look at Eric Coffman. After knowing each other in college, the two men had met professionally in what was at first an adversarial relationship, Lindsey representing International Surety, Coffman acting as attorney for a disgruntled beneficiary. After the case was settled Lindsey and Coffman had become good friends, and Coffman had become Lindsey's personal attorney as well.

Coffman knew about Marvia and Willie Fergus. He was the first — and only — person Lindsey had told about Marvia's decision. He'd offered a sympathetic shoulder for Lindsey to cry on, and had offered to take him out and get him good and drunk if that would help, but Lindsey had turned down the invitation.

The talk was mainly of Mother's impending marriage to Gordon Sloane. Sloane was spending the evening with his own grown son and daughter. They would meet in the morning. The wedding would take place in the garden at Sloane's married daughter's house.

Coffman avoided mentioning Marvia during the meal, and he had obviously coached Miriam to do the same. But when Miriam left the table to fetch the main course from her kitchen, Rebecca asked, 'Why didn't Jamie come along? We thought he was coming along, didn't we, Sarah?'

'We were going to show him our new

Nintendo cartridges,' Sarah said.

Eric Coffman caught Lindsey's eye. This time it was male telepathy rather than female telepathy. Lindsey telepathed back, *It's all right, it's nobody's fault.* Aloud he said, 'Jamie is with his grandma tonight.'

'Where's his mom?' Rebecca demanded. 'Where's Ms. Plum?'

Lindsey said, 'She couldn't come tonight. You know, she's a police officer. They can't always make their own schedules.' Rebecca and Sarah seemed to accept that.

Eric Coffman said to Mother, 'Bart tells me you're going to honeymoon in Hawaii.'

She picked up on that and began describing her honeymoon plans. She sounded as happy as a bride.

Miriam Coffman reappeared. The evening went on.

Driving home to Walnut Creek, Lindsey didn't play another cassette. He turned on the radio, low, to a classical station and ignored the music.

Apparently Mother hadn't picked up

on the by-play about Marvia, or maybe she knew more than she seemed to know and chose to keep her own counsel. When they got back to Walnut Creek, she asked Lindsey to drive once around the block, just for a quiet look. 'You know,' she said, 'I've lived in this neighborhood for forty years. We moved here when you were a tiny baby. Just you and me, Hobo. I never thought of leaving Laurel Drive.'

He pulled into their driveway and helped Mother from the car. She stood in front of the house, looking at it in the pale light of the night. 'It's like the end of my life,' she said.

'No, Mother. Don't — it isn't.'

She smiled and reached up to pat his cheek, something she'd done ten thousand times in the past. 'I'm not sad. Only a little, anyway. I'm starting a new life, I know.'

'Yes, you are.'

They went inside the house and she made hot chocolate for them both, even though neither felt the need for it after Miriam Coffman's generous dinner; it gave them an excuse to stay up and to stay in each other's company a while longer. When they'd finished the chocolate, Mother pressed her cheek to Lindsey's and held him before she went to bed. He stayed up and washed out their cups, then turned on the TV, then turned it off again, then sat in the living room with the lights turned off for a while, before going to bed.

★　★　★

The wedding was flawless. Credit Sloane for that. The groom's daughter and her husband lived in a huge new house in Danville, surrounded by millionaire athletes and successful investors. The garden was filled with early-blooming roses. A rose-covered arbor had been decorated for the wedding party to stand beneath during the ceremony.

The groom's best man was his son. Mother had asked Lindsey to give her away. 'Isn't it a funny custom, Hobo? You'd think men owned women. How can anybody give someone else away?' But he said he'd be happy to do it, if that was what she wanted.

The whole Coffman family were present, and Mrs. Hernandez, Mother's one-time babysitter from the bad days when she'd wandered the corridors of time searching forlornly for the door into the past. Joanie Schorr, no longer little Joanie Schorr but a beautiful young pre-med student, kissed Lindsey's mother and cried a little.

Lindsey was astonished when he met the officiating clergyman. He wore a blue suit and a solid maroon necktie and a white yarmulke. He was an old friend of Miriam and Eric Coffman's and referred to the groom as Gershon ben Moishe, explaining that Gordon Sloane, née Slonimsky, had asked him to use his Hebrew name for the wedding ceremony.

You learn something every day. Lindsey had never been to a Jewish wedding before, and would never have dreamed that when the day came, it would be his Mother's.

After the ceremony, Lindsey stood chatting with Mrs. Hernandez, a glass of champagne in his hand. He felt a tap on the shoulder and whirled around, slopping a little champagne on the well-tended lawn.

'Hoholindo!'

Nobody had called him Hoholindo since junior high. The woman was as tall as Lindsey was, big-boned, with curly hair that might have been platinum-blonde or premature white. She wore a picture hat straight out of an Alice Faye movie, and a flowered chiffon dress that showed off an attractively Junoesque figure. Her makeup was also done in the 1940s style — dark red lipstick, mascara and rouge. Lindsey blinked.

'Don't you remember me?' The woman's voice was familiar, and once he heard it he did remember her. 'Artie? Artemis Janson?'

'That's right. It's been a few other things over the years, but it's Janson again now. I'm a friend of Gordo Slonimsky's. I heard he was getting hitched again, but I never imagined the blushing bride was your mama. She must have got over her — well, she looks wonderful, Lindo.'

Lindsey turned back to introduce

Artemis to Mrs. Hernandez, but Mrs. Hernandez had moved off into the crowd. To Artemis, Lindsey said, 'I can't remember the last time I saw you. It must have been — '

'I remember it.' Artemis lifted the champagne glass from Lindsey's hand. 'You don't mind, do you?' She drank part of the champagne, then returned the glass to him. 'I remember it very well. Golden Gate Park. Summer of 1967. Summer of Love.' He found himself blushing. 'We were both fourteen, and we hitchhiked into the city and went to a free concert in the park. Jefferson Airplane was playing. Everybody was smoking dope and that guru type in the Mr. Natural robe offered us a joint. Don't tell me you don't remember that.' She borrowed his glass and finished the champagne. 'Don't go away.' She took a half-dozen long strides, put the empty glass down on a linen-covered serving table, and returned with two full ones.

Lindsey said, 'I guess I remember.' In fact he remembered very well.

'Where did you go? One minute we

were turning on and the Airplane was playing and everything was just amazing and wonderful — and when I looked around, you were gone.'

'I went home to Walnut Creek. The big question, Artie, was, where did *you* go? You didn't come back to Walnut Creek, then and nobody saw you for six months; and when you did come back, you'd never tell anybody what you'd been doing.'

'I'll tell you all about it some time. I'm just so happy that we met again. Lindo, do you still live in that little house on Laurel Drive? I haven't set foot in Walnut Creek in twenty years. I've been all over — lived in Europe for a while, then in Japan, got married two or three times. You see that beautiful creature over there?' She indicated a slim young woman in a bright orange dress that came to the top of her thighs. Two men were competing for her attention. 'My daughter. By my second husband. What a handful she is! But what have you been up to? Are you married? What do you think of your mother tying the knot again at her age?'

Lindsey started to explain but Artemis Janson took him by the wrist and led him away from the milling crowd. 'We have so much catching up to do! Finding you after all these years — I'm not going to let go of you again.'

*　*　*

Lindsey slept that night in the Laurel Drive house, the first time in his life that he had slept there alone, without at least expecting to see Mother in the morning. The house was silent. He would fall asleep, wake up, prowl around for a while, then climb back into bed.

*　*　*

As the 737 jet came down into an icy and wind-blown Denver International Airport, it was Lindsey's first look at the new airport. On a day like this it didn't look any different from the old Stapleton.

Walking through the lobby, he caught sight of Cletus Berry and waved to his

348

one-time roommate and SPUDS colleague. They shared a cab into town and picked up their reservations at the Embassy Suites on Curtis Street. Lindsey recognized several former classmates. It looked as if his class of SPUDS trainees had fared better than most — or maybe the fabled high rate of attrition among SPUDS operatives was a legend, carefully fostered by Desmond Richelieu to keep his troops on their toes.

Lindsey and Berry shared a suite, as they had shared a room during SPUDS training. The refresher course was scheduled to start Tuesday morning and run for four days. Lindsey phoned the desk and asked if Aurora Delano or Gina Rossellini had checked in yet. Both of them had, and Lindsey invited them to join Berry and himself for dinner.

None of them knew Denver well, but Lindsey had consulted a guidebook and settled on an establishment called Morton's of Chicago. He was in a Chicago mood, he decided, after his adventures in the Vansittart case. And he loved the guidebook's description of Morton's: 'a tavern for the wealthy.' The prices were not as breathtaking as they might have been, and this trip was on expenses anyway. SPUDS agents got the toughest cases in International Surety — they were expected to save the company large sums of money — and in exchange the company could afford to feed them well.

Rossellini, Berry and Delano had all helped Lindsey solve the Vansittart mystery. All three stood to share in Lindsey's glory, if only in a small way, for having saved International Surety $1,000,000. All had access to KlameNet/Plus and knew what the KNP file on Vansittart contained.

Lindsey filled them in, in more detail, on the varied aspects of the case. He asked Berry about Lovisi, the publisher.

Berry grinned. 'He sure is a character! I went to his place out in Brooklyn and he showed me his collection of paperbacks. You wouldn't believe what the man has.'

'Yes, I would, if it's anything like Scotty Anderson's collection in California.'

Neither Gina Rossellini nor Aurora Delano had ever encountered a serious case of the collecting bug. They were suitably fascinated by Berry's description of Lovisi and Lindsey's description of Anderson. The two collectors were different physical types and had different personalities, but they were brothers beneath the skin. Lindsey wondered what the famous Lovisi would say when he saw Anderson's photos of the Paige paperbacks, and when he learned that Anderson now owned a complete set of the books.

Over coffee, Aurora told Lindsey that she was keeping up with the Bruninskis. 'It's really sad.' She gazed into her cup. 'That woman stayed with her husband all these years — more than forty years, closer to fifty now — living like fugitives, poor as church mice. Now she's a millionaire, and what good does it do her? She lies in bed all day.' She shuddered. 'I think I'd rather be dead.' She shook like a dog coming out of a stream. 'Let's talk about something else. The bad guy, what's his name, ben Zinowicz — he's back in California, right?'

'He is, indeed. And it's going to be a

long time before he sees the outside of a jail cell, if he ever does. The only question is who gets his services, San Quentin prison or the US Attorney's office. He killed O'Farrell, not much question about that. Is it worth cutting a deal with ben Zinowicz to hang the Cookes? Or will the Cookes turn on ben Zinowicz and hope to make a deal themselves?' He picked an after-dinner mint off a silver tray and slowly unwrapped it. Something cold and sad inside him thought, *Jamie would like this*.

Aurora Delano read his mind. 'Are you still with Marvia, Bart? She's wonderful; I just loved her when you were down in Louisiana together. She was terrific on that trip out to Reserve. I don't think anybody could have got the info that she did.'

Lindsey bit his lower lip. 'We're no longer together.'

'Oh, I'm so sorry.' Aurora put her hand on the back of Lindsey's wrist. 'I hope nothing — I mean, did you break up? Police work is dangerous, I know . . . '

'Nothing like that.' Lindsey looked at

his wristwatch. 'You know, there's that little welcoming ceremony in the morning, Ducky Richelieu likes people to arrive on time with a clean, pressed suit and a bright, fresh grin.' Cletus Berry called for the check.

Back at the Embassy Suites, Cletus headed straight for the elevator. Gina Rossellini smiled at Lindsey. 'You're right, Bart, it is late, but I'm just so jangled up, airplanes do that to me. What say to a nightcap?'

Aurora Delano was standing a few feet away. Gina said, 'You're included, too, Aurora. Of course.'

Aurora turned angrily and walked to the elevator.

* * *

Lindsey did all right during the days. It was the nights that were hard to get through. After Monday night's celebration at Morton's there were working dinners every evening, and informal sessions afterwards. The director was there every day and every evening, and he

353

wanted to have a quiet, one-to-one chat with each of his operatives.

Cletus Berry's turn came Tuesday night. There seemed to be no pattern to the sequence of meetings. You just went when the director called. Richelieu had got his pre-International Surety training in the FBI during the last years of the J. Edgar Hoover regime. Sometimes he seemed to think he was Hoover *redivivus*.

Lindsey was sitting at a desk in the Embassy Suites, preparing for Wednesday's seminars, when Berry returned from his meeting with Richelieu. Lindsey looked up at his roommate. 'Well?' he said.

'The director is one strange man, you know that, Bart? He wanted to know what I thought of the mayor, what I thought of the governor, whether I thought the Bronx would ever become a desirable site for a major real estate development, and what I thought of . . . Hobart Lindsey.'

'And?'

'I told him that the mayor was doing a

better job than I expected; that the governor was caught between Washington, Albany, and New York City and there was no way he could win; and that the Bronx would surely recover someday, but we'd all be dead and gone before that day ever arrived.'

Lindsey said, 'I think I'll watch the headlines and hit the sack.'

Berry sighed. 'Okay, I couldn't resist the temptation. What the hell should I tell the director? You're one odd duck, Bart. You wander into the goddamnedest cases I've ever heard of, not just one or two of them but a whole parade of the wacko things. Every time I see your name on KNP I know it's going to be something odd. Every time I get a message from you I know it's going to be a bizarre case. But they're always interesting, and you always manage to solve them and save the company big bucks. Ducky Richelieu calls you his private Sherlock Holmes. I guess he's right.'

'I don't always save the company money,' Lindsey demurred. 'Did you see the final report on the settlement we had

to make on that B-17 a few years ago?
Everyone wanted money from us, even
the navy. And they collected, too.'

'Okay, I remember that case. I heard a
lot about it. How could I help it? You
made all the papers and the TV shows
and the news mags. You were the one who
talked that guy into trying to land on the
aircraft carrier, otherwise the little boy
would have died with him. You were a
hero.'

'Some hero,' Lindsey said.

'Anyway, Ducky isn't quite sure what
to make of you. I think he might offer you
a job as his personal troubleshooter.
You're too dangerous to have running
around loose and you're too valuable to
dump. I think he wants to keep you
around on a short chain.' Berry was
pacing back and forth on the thick carpet.
Now he halted, standing over Lindsey.
'What will you tell him? If he offers that,
what will you tell him?'

Lindsey stood up and faced Berry. 'I
don't have the remotest idea what I'd tell
him.' He snorted. 'And you can quote me
on that.'

Lindsey's meeting with Richelieu came Wednesday night after a working dinner and a short pep talk by a faceless functionary from corporate staff. Richelieu had set up a temporary office at the Embassy Suites — he didn't want people orbiting between the conference and his permanent office overlooking Cherry Creek.

Richelieu's makeshift headquarters was an ordinary hotel room, the bed removed and replaced by living room furniture. Room service provided coffee and brandy. Richelieu acted the expansive host. 'You're a star again,' he greeted Lindsey.

'Do I get a private trailer?'

Richelieu laughed. 'Very good. I don't think so. How are you doing at the conference? Three days down, one to go. Are we giving you useful stuff? Any complaints? Anything you need that you're not getting?'

Lindsey shook his head. 'It's good info. The legal types had a lot to say. And the KNP enhancement program looks good.

Pretty soon we'll all be able to sit at our computers and never leave the house. Sounds like a sci-fi writer's dream world.'

Richelieu exhaled. 'I don't think so.' He stood up, coffee cup in hand. He added some brandy to his cup, held the bottle toward Lindsey, and poured dark amber liqueur into the coffee. 'I've been watching you, Lindsey. You're racking up quite a record. This latest save was really something. Your name has been mentioned in high places; spoken trippingly on the tongues of the high and the mighty.' Richelieu rolled his eyeballs heavenward. Behind his glinting gold-rimmed glasses, they looked like shimmering marbles. 'So we have to ask, what are we going to do with you?'

Lindsey was ready for that, thanks to Cletus Berry. 'What do you want to do, Mr. Richelieu?'

Richelieu had lowered the brandy bottle. Now he raised his coffee cup and sipped. 'Lindsey, do you like Denver?'

'Not especially.'

'How would you like to work out of my

office, reporting directly to me and only to me?'

'I like my work now.'

Richelieu put his cup down hard. 'You don't lick anybody's boots, do you, Lindsey?'

'No, I don't.'

'Are you turning down my offer?'

'I haven't heard one.'

Richelieu focused on Lindsey's face. 'There's hardly a soul in this company who doesn't tremble at the sound of my name, did you know that? And you act as if you just don't care.' He paused but Lindsey did not reply. 'That's why you scare me, Lindsey. It's also why I like you.'

Lindsey conceded a small smile. 'Thanks.'

'All right. Meeting over. I'll see you at the seminar tomorrow.'

Lindsey stood up. He hadn't touched his coffee since Richelieu added the brandy to it.

Richelieu tapped Lindsey's coffee cup with a carefully manicured fingernail. 'You're not that worried, are you? That

I'd doctor your coffee?'

'Of course you wouldn't.' He shook Richelieu's hand.

Thursday was another day of lectures and exercises. More KNP enhancements were coming down the road. Corporate staff was counting on SPUDS to act as the vanguard for cutting-edge corporate technology. Lindsey felt as if a heavy-weight boxer was pounding rhythmically at his head, first a left to the right ear, then a right to the left ear . . .

That night the TV news showed a well-dressed Roger St. John Cooke and Cynthia Cooke being taken into custody by federal agents. The announcer explained that they were being charged with multiple charges of conspiracy, fraud and tax evasion. The Cookes had nothing to say, but their lawyer, decked out in his thousand-dollar hand-tailored suit and hundred-dollar silk tie, insisted that his clients were totally innocent of any wrongdoing save decades of service to the artistic community of America. The government had no case whatsoever and the Cookes would be fully

360

vindicated when the facts were known. There was no mention of Albert Crocker Vansittart, John O'Farrell, or Nathan ben Zinowicz. Marge Tillotson appeared briefly and told a reporter that she would present her case fully at the appropriate time and asked to be excused.

Cletus Berry stood behind Lindsey's easy chair, watching the news broadcast. 'Those friends of yours, Hobart?'

Lindsey said, 'I know them. They aren't my friends.'

★   ★   ★

Friday was the last day of the seminar. A group of SPUDS agents assembled at the Palace Arms a couple of hours after the last session. There was no graduation ceremony this time, no valedictory speeches or pep talks from corporate chieftains; just an exchange of hopes and plans, and a series of goodbyes and perfunctory promises to keep in touch.

Leaving the restaurant, Gina Rossellini invited Lindsey to her room for a nightcap. She'd lucked out with the arrangements, or maybe she knew somebody in the assistant manager's office. At any rate, her quarters at the Embassy Suites included a fireplace and a bottle of brandy and even a CD player.

The music might have been furnished by the management, but more likely, Lindsey surmised, Gina had brought it with her from Chicago. Her taste ran to lush orchestrations of familiar tunes that he could almost, but not quite, name. Her roommate, if she had one, was nowhere in evidence. Lindsey wondered for a moment where she was; then he wondered if Cletus Berry was worried about him. He decided that Berry wouldn't give a damn, and he didn't give a damn about Gina's roommate. The fire crackled, the brandy was splendid, and outside the Embassy Suites a few snowflakes were drifting from sky to street.

Gina had worn something in midnight blue to dinner, with a broad v-neck. Her raven hair swept over one shoulder and onto her chest. Lindsey realized that his first glimpse of her in Chicago, his first take on her, had been unfair. She was no young girl, and she had taken her share of life's hard knocks, that much was obvious. But she was a survivor. She was the kind to get back up when life knocked her down, and here in a hotel room a thousand miles from either of their homes, she was an attractive woman.

She touched Lindsey's hand. 'Bart? Are you all right?'

He blinked. 'I'm sorry. Did you ask something?'

'I asked about your plans. Not the stuff everybody was bullshitting about at the restaurant. This is just the two of us. What are you going to do?'

He raised his brandy snifter and held it before his eyes. 'My job,' he said.

They were seated side by side on a sofa. Gina leaned toward him and brushed the side of his neck with her fingers. 'Come on, Lindsey, you're too old to play coy. You've been dumped. What are you going to do?'

He looked into his brandy snifter for an answer but he couldn't see one there.

'You're headed out of here in the morning, back to Pecan Patch, California, right?'

She was close to Lindsey and he was finding the sensation pleasant. He blinked at the carpet in front of the couch and saw that she'd kicked off her shoes. He liked the sight of her feet. 'Walnut Creek,' he corrected her.

'And I'm headed back to Chicago. And here we are at a corporate conference. It's a classic, isn't it?'

Lindsey watched her silhouette moving between him and the fireplace. The music could have been less corny, but what the hell, it wasn't *that* bad.

She said, 'If you don't start doing something I'm going to cry for help.'

He said, 'Promise you'll still respect me in the morning.'

★ ★ ★

In the morning Lindsey made a call to Desmond Richelieu's private number. He got the director, sounding wide awake and chipper as ever.

Lindsey said, 'I'll take it.'

The director said, 'Go home and start packing. Call Mrs. Blomquist for details.'

Richelieu hung up.

* * *

A few hours later, Lindsey arrived at his house on Laurel Drive. Mother and Gordon Sloane were in Hawaii and Joanie Schorr had kindly brought in a week's worth of mail and put it on the dining room table.

Before he looked at the mail he checked the telephone answering machine. There were several messages from Marge Tillotson at the US Attorney's office. He'd have to follow up on the Cookes and ben Zinowicz, but already the Vansittart case seemed like part of a life that he'd lived on another planet.

There was a message from Artie Janson inviting him to call her and catch up on their lives. There was even a message from Mother and Gordon Sloane, having a grand time in Hawaii and hoping to see him when they got home. Nothing that couldn't wait.

The mail consisted of an assortment of bills and ads and a single personal item. It came in a square envelope with a Reno postmark. Lindsey tried to tear it open but his fingers were suddenly stiff and numb. He got a kitchen knife instead, slit the envelope, and read exactly what he expected and exactly what he feared: a printed announcement of the marriage of Willie Fergus and Marvia Plum Wilkerson. He turned the announcement over and saw a hand-written message in greenish-blue ink. It was from Marvia, and it said that she was sorry she'd hurt him and she would love him forever and hoped that someday they could be friends.

He felt tired and had a headache. He dropped his suit coat on the back of a chair and walked past the TV on his way to the kitchen. He poured himself a glass of orange juice and drank half of it. He felt better at once.

He carried the glass back to the living room and stood in front of the TV. A black-and-white photograph of his father, surrounded by a red-white-and-blue frame, stood on the set. How many times had he walked past that photo, yet never really seen it? He wondered: had he deliberately kept it out of his consciousness, aware at some level that the thoughts it would inspire would be too painful to endure?

But now — but now . . .

Joseph Lindsey looked ridiculously young in the photo — like a high school boy, decked out in a dark blue navy uniform, white sailor's cap cocked at a jaunty angle, a grin on his face. He could have passed for a stand-in for Gene Kelly in *On the Town*. Hobart Lindsey picked up the picture and read the inscription: *To my Darling Wife. I'll be back soon! With all my love — Joey!*

Joey. Lindsey shivered. Joey had never come back from Korea. His darling wife was already pregnant by then, pregnant with Hobart Lindsey. He'd never got to meet his father, never got to know him. All he had was this picture.

He put it back on the TV and settled in

his favorite chair. Joey's darling wife was now Mrs. Gordon Sloane, and bless her and her new husband for whatever happiness lay ahead of them. But what about Lindsey himself?

Marvia Plum, who had been so much a part of his life, was gone now, gone to be the wife of a sheriff's deputy in Nevada. Nathan ben Zinowicz was locked away, probably for the rest of his life. Roger and Cynthia Cooke, too, would pay the penalty for running their crooked charity. Benjamin Bruninsky and Maizie Cartowicz, better known as the painter Ben Brown and his favorite model, Mae Carter, would at least live in a degree of comfort for their remaining days.

And Lindsey himself? He felt suddenly empty, bewildered. Everything that had given his life meaning was gone. He was vested in International Surety's retirement plan. He could take early retirement, cash out, sell the house and — what? Look for another job? Grow a beard, move to an island in the Pacific, become a beach-comber?

He shook his head and laughed aloud

at himself. Maybe twenty years ago. It was too late for that now. He'd already accepted Desmond Richelieu's offer of a position as his deputy. The new job meant a major promotion and a proportionate bump in his salary. Aside from the material rewards, it represented at least a tacit acknowledgment of his past achievements and his contributions to International Surety.

On the other hand, it would mean saying goodbye to the home and the area where he'd lived all his life, to the neighbors he'd grown up with, and to his friends. Could he really say goodbye to Eric Coffman and his pleasant wife and their adorable children, children to whom he had been an honorary uncle for many years? Could he write off his renewed friendship with Artemis Janson?

Lindsey stood up, felt in his pocket and pulled out a coin. He flipped it in the air, caught it, and slid it back into his pocket without looking at it. What a stupid way to make a decision. This was ridiculous. He'd already made up his mind. This was no time for buyer's remorse. Walnut

Creek was the past. His new job in Denver was the future.

He drank down the rest of his orange juice, crossed to the TV set and returned its controls to their default settings. He settled into his easy chair again, clicked on the remote and surfed to a movie channel. They were showing *The Caine Mutiny*. Lindsey had seen it before. At one time Mother had insisted that she'd seen Joey playing an extra on the minesweeper *Caine*. 'Look, look, Hobo, look my little Hobo, there's your dad!' All he saw was a long shot of sailors lining the rail of a battered World War II minesweeper. At this distance their faces were blobs.

At Mother's insistence they'd always watched the film together, watched it with the TV controls set to black and white. This time, for the first time, Lindsey watched the film in color.

We do hope that you have enjoyed reading this large print book.

Did you know that all of our titles are available for purchase?

We publish a wide range of high quality large print books including:
**Romances, Mysteries, Classics
General Fiction
Non Fiction and Westerns**

Special interest titles available in large print are:
**The Little Oxford Dictionary
Music Book, Song Book
Hymn Book, Service Book**

Also available from us courtesy of Oxford University Press:
**Young Readers' Dictionary
(large print edition)
Young Readers' Thesaurus
(large print edition)**

For further information or a free brochure, please contact us at:
**Ulverscroft Large Print Books Ltd.,
The Green, Bradgate Road, Anstey,
Leicester, LE7 7FU, England.
Tel:** (00 44) **0116 236 4325
Fax:** (00 44) **0116 234 0205**

THE BODY IN THE SWAMP

Ardath Mayhar

When several bodies are washed up in the swamplands of east Texas, the local police suspect drug-runners, and the Feds are called in to investigate — but can discover little. Possum Choa lives off the fat of the land, but his way of life is now threatened by the criminals infesting the area. With the help of his old friend Lena McCarver, possessed of mysterious powers of her own, and Police Chief Washington Shipp, Choa and the residents of the swamplands join forces to stop the evildoers once and for all.

A QUESTION OF GUILT

Tony Gleeson

Dane Spilwell, a brilliant surgeon, stands accused of the brutal murder of his wife. The evidence against him is damning, his guilt almost a foregone conclusion. Two red-haired women will determine his ultimate fate. One, a mysterious lady in emeralds, may be the key to clearing him of the crime — if only she can be located. The other, Detective Jilly Garvey, began by doggedly working to convict him — but now finds herself doubting his culpability . . .

TWEAK THE DEVIL'S NOSE

Richard Deming

Driving to the El Patio club to see his girlfriend Fausta Moreni, the establishment's proprietor, private investigator Manville Moon does not expect to be witness to a murder. As he steps from his car outside the club, he hears a gun suddenly roar from the bushes close behind him. Walter Lancaster, the lieutenant governor of the neighbouring state of Illinois, has been shot! The assassination will not only make headlines all over the country, but also place the lives of Moon and Fausta in deadly danger . . .

THE MAN WITH THE CAMERA EYES

Victor Rousseau

Investigative lawyer Langton has solved many bizarre cases with the help of his friend Peter Crewe, who possesses such an extraordinary photographic memory that he never forgets a face. Here Langton relates twelve stories featuring audacious jewel robberies, scientific geniuses gone mad and bad, and cold-blooded murder served up via amusement park rides, craftily concealed explosives, and hot air balloons. In each, the Man with the Camera Eyes provides the observations and deductions that are crucial to the solution of the mystery — often risking his own life in the process . . .

THE SEPIA SIREN KILLER

Richard A. Lupoff

Prior to World War II, black actors were restricted to minor roles in mainstream films — though there was a 'black' Hollywood that created films with all-black casts for exhibition to black audiences. When a cache of long-lost films is discovered by cinema researchers, the aged director Edward 'Speedy' MacReedy appears to reclaim his place in film history. But insurance investigator Hobart Lindsey and homicide officer Marvia Plum soon find themselves enmeshed in a frightening web of arson and murder with its roots deep in the tragic events of a past era . . .